YES MINISTER

In the same series
Yes Minister: Volume One

YES MINISTER

THE DIARIES OF A CABINET MINISTER
BY THE RT HON. JAMES HACKER MP

Volume Two

*Edited by Jonathan Lynn
and Antony Jay*

BRITISH BROADCASTING CORPORATION

Published by the
British Broadcasting Corporation
35 Marylebone High Street
London W1M 4AA

ISBN 0 563 20065 0
First published 1982
Reprinted 1983 (twice)

© Jonathan Lynn and Antony Jay 1982

Typeset by Phoenix Photosetting, Chatham
Printed in England
by Mackays of Chatham Ltd

Contents

Editors' Note

This is the second volume of the *Diaries of A Cabinet Minister*. James Hacker kept his diaries from the day on which he first entered the Cabinet. He dictated them into his tape-recorder, sometimes on a daily basis, more often at weekends in his constituency home.

His original plan had simply been to take notes for his memoirs. But he soon realised the intrinsic interest of a diary which would give a daily picture of the struggles of a Cabinet Minister.

Naturally there are discrepancies in his account of events – both within the book itself, and when compared objectively with outside events. Being a journalist, he had no particular talent for reporting facts.

Furthermore, when the diaries were first transcribed, they were hardly readable, having been dictated very much *ad lib*, rather like his polytechnic lectures. (Hacker, you will remember, was initially a polytechnic lecturer before he became editor of *Reform* and entered politics.) There is also much boring repetition, as you would expect from a politician, and relevant passages do not necessarily occur in chronological order. Or in any discernible order, logical or chronological.

He always intended to rewrite the diaries with a view to improving the clarity, accuracy and relevance of his publication. Towards the end of his life, however, he abandoned that plan because he saw no reason why he should be the only politician publishing memoirs which adhered to those criteria.

The editors have therefore had to undertake that task, and also remove the very many references to his closest friends and colleagues which were either libellous or in very poor taste.

Hacker had been in what he liked to call power for only four months by the time what turned out to be Volume One of the *Diaries* was completed. This volume covers the next few months, and it will be seen that he was gradually acquiring greater skill in dealing with his chief civil servant, Sir Humphrey Appleby, the Permanent Under-Secretary of the Department of Administrative Affairs.

Again we should like to acknowledge our debt to Sir Humphrey Appleby who gave us such help as he could during his last few lucid moments, and to Sir Bernard Woolley, GCB, (Hacker's private secretary at the time these diaries were written) who subsequently became Head of the Home Civil Service. Most valuable of all are the many papers which became available to us under the 30-year rule.

We encountered three principle problem areas in the editing process: chronological, technical and interpretation. First, chronology. At all times we have striven to maintain a chronological day by day account of each of the main events that he retells, even though the original diaries are much more confused. There is a risk of historical inaccuracy in this approach, as Hacker himself was indeed deeply confused for most of his time in office, and the diaries perhaps ought to reflect this confusion. If, however, the diaries reflected his confusion in full, they would become virtually incomprehensible to the reader – as, indeed, the events themselves often were to Hacker.

Technically we have completed and punctuated sentences, unmixed the metaphors and corrected the grammar, unless by leaving the original we can give an insight into Hacker's state of mind.

Finally, interpretation. Where the book is ambiguous, we have assumed that this is a deliberate exercise of his political skills. Often he was unclear about what events meant, but often he was deliberately vague. These diaries accurately reflect the mind of one of our outstanding national leaders. If the reflection seems clouded, it may not be the fault of the mirror.

Jonathan Lynn
Antony Jay
Hacker College, Oxford.
July, 2018 AD

1

The Compassionate Society

March 1st

Having effectively squashed the awful scandal that was brewing over the Solihull project,[1] but having done a deal with Frank Weisel on the little matter of his suggested reforms in the Quango system as a price for extricating myself from the appalling mess that Humphrey had got me into, I decided this weekend to consider my various options.

First of all it has become clear that Frank has to go. He really is very uncouth and, valuable as he was to me during my days in opposition, I can see that he lacks the subtlety, skill and discretion that my professional advisers display constantly.

[*The contradiction inherent in these two paragraphs indicates the state of mental confusion in which Hacker now found himself about Sir Humphrey after five months in Whitehall – Ed.*]

However, having despatched the self-righteously incorruptible Frank the day before yesterday on his arduous fact-finding mission to review important centres of government – California, Jamaica, and Tahiti – I already feel a load off my mind as one significant source of pressure on me is lifted. I felt free and easy for the first time in months, as if I had actually gained time yesterday. [*As it was a leap year, he actually had gained time yesterday – Ed.*]

I am now able to draw some conclusions about the Civil Service in general and Sir Humphrey in particular. I begin to see that senior civil servants in the open structure[2] have, surprisingly enough, almost as brilliant minds as they themselves would claim to have. However, since there are virtually no goals or targets that can be achieved by a civil servant personally, his high IQ is usually devoted

[1] See *Yes Minister* Volume One, page 166.
[2] The 800 people with the rank of Under-Secretary and above.

to the avoidance of error.

Civil servants are posted to new jobs every three years or so. This is supposed to gain them all-round experience on the way to the top. In practice, it merely ensures that they can never have any personal interest in achieving the success of a policy: a policy of any complexity takes longer than three years to see through from start to finish, so a civil servant either has to leave it before its passage is completed or he arrives on the scene long after it started. This also means you can never pin the blame for failure on any individual: the man in charge at the end will say it was started wrong, and the man in charge at the beginning will say it was finished wrong.

Curiously the Civil Service seem to approve of this system. They don't like civil servants to become emotionally involved in the success or failure of policies. Policies are for Ministers. Ministers or Governments stand or fall by them. Civil servants see themselves as public-spirited impartial advisers attempting to implement, with total impartiality, whatever policy the Minister or the Government see fit.

Except that they *don't*, do they? There's the rub.

Because Permanent Secretaries are always trying to steer Ministers of all parties towards 'the common ground'. [*In other words, the Department's policy – a policy they have some hope of being able to pursue uninterrupted, whichever party is in power – Ed.*]

Afterthought: considering that the avoidance of error is their main priority, it is surprising how many errors they make!

March 2nd

Today, Sunday, has been spent going through my boxes and mugging up on my PQs [*Parliamentary Questions – Ed.*] for tomorrow.

I take PQs very seriously, as do all Ministers with any sense. Although the voters are mainly aware of a Minister's activities through the newspapers and television, his real power and influence still stems from the House of Commons. A Minister cannot afford to make an idiot of himself in the House, and will not last long if he doesn't learn to perform there adequately.

One day a month this ghastly event takes place. PQs are the modern equivalent of throwing the Christians to the lions, or the medieval ordeal by combat. One day a month I'm on First Order, and some other Minister from some other Department is on Second Order. Another day, vice versa. [*There's also Third Order but no one knows what it's there for because its never been reached –Ed.*]

The Sundays and Mondays before I'm on First Order are absolute bloody anguish. I should think they're anguish for the civil servants too. Bernard, my Private Secretary, has an Assistant Private Secretary employed full-time on getting answers together for all possible supplementaries. Legions of civil servants sit around Whitehall exercising their feverish imaginations, trying to foretell what possible supplementaries could be coming from the backbenchers. Usually, of course, I can guess the political implications of a PQ better than my civil servants.

Then, when the gruesome moment arrives you stand up in the House – which is usually packed as it's just after lunch, and PQs are considered good clean fun because there's always a chance that a Minister will humiliate himself.

Still, I'm reasonably relaxed this evening, secure in the knowledge that, as always, I am thoroughly prepared for Question Time tomorrow. One thing I'm proud of is that, no matter how Sir Humphrey makes rings round me in administrative matters,[1] I have always prided myself on my masterful control over the House.

March 3rd

I can hardly believe it. PQs today were a disaster! A totally unforeseen catastrophe. Although I did manage to snatch a sort of Pyrrhic victory from the jaws of defeat. I came in bright and early and went over all the possible supplementaries – I thought! – and spent lunchtime being tested by Bernard.

The first question was from Jim Lawford of Birmingham South-West who had asked me about the government's pledge to reduce the number of administrators in the Health Service.

I gave the prepared reply, which was a little self-congratulatory – to the civil servants who wrote it, of course, not to me!

[*We have found the relevant exchange in Hansard, and reprint it overleaf – Ed.*]

---

[1] A sign of growing awareness here from Hacker.

The Minister of Administrative Affairs (Mr. James Hacker): The Government has already achieved a reduction of 11·3% in administrative and clerical staff and is actually pursuing further economies. And in view of low pay and low morale and the fact that our health administrators are constantly under attack, I would like to take this opportunity to congratulate them on the vital contribution they make to the smooth running of the Health Service.

Mr. Lawford: I'm sure the house will welcome the Minister's tribute. I am aware it was actually written for him by his health administrators, but all the same he read it out beautifully. [Opposition laughter] But would the Minister explain how his assurance to the House squares with this minute from his own department. I quote: "We are concerned at the increase of 7% in Administrative and Clerical staff. However, if data processing staff were reclassified from 'administrative' to 'technical' [HON. MEMBERS: "Oh!"] if secretarial staff in hospitals were redesignated as 'ancillary workers' [HON. MEMBERS: "Oh!"] and if the base of comparison was charged from the financial to the calendar year, then the figures would show a fall of 11·3%." Would the Minister care to comment on this shabby deception?

Hon. Members: Answer! Answer!

Somebody had leaked this wretched paper to Lawford. He was waving it about with a kind of wild glee, his fat face shining with excitement. Everyone was shouting for an answer. Humphrey – or somebody – had been up to his old tricks again, disguising an increase in the numbers of administrative and secretarial staff simply by calling them by some other name. But a rose by any other name is still a rose, as Wordsworth said. [*In fact, Shakespeare said 'A rose by any other name would smell as sweet.' But Hacker was an ex-journalist and Polytechnic Lecturer – Ed.*] This looked like it was going to be a real political stink. And a stink by any other name is still a stink. [*Or a stink by any other name would smell as bad? – Ed.*] Had it stayed secret, it would have been seen as a brilliant manoeuvre to pass off an increase of staff by 7% as a decrease of 11.3% – but when leaked, it suddenly comes into the category of a shabby deception. What's more, an *unsuccessful* shabby deception – quite the worst kind!

I stalled rather well in the circumstances:

Hon. Members: Answer! Answer!

Mr. James Hacker: I have no knowledge of the document which the Honorable Member is brandishing. [Opposition jeers and cries of "why not?"]

Mr. Lawford: I will happily give the date and file reference to the Minister in exchange for an assurance that he will set up a full independent enquiry.

[Opposition cheers.]

Mr. Hacker: I will be very happy to look into the matter. [Opposition cries of "cover-up", "resign" and "whitewash."]

Thank God one of my own backbenchers came to my rescue. Gerry Chandler asked me if I could reassure my friends that the enquiries would not be carried out by my own department but by an independent investigator who would command the respect of the House. I was forced to say that I was happy to give that assurance.

So I just about satisfied the House on that one. However, I shall have to have a very serious talk about the whole matter with Humphrey and Bernard tomorrow. I don't mind the deception, but allowing me to look ridiculous at Question Time is simply not on!

It's not even in *their* interest – I wasn't able to defend the Department, was I?

March 4th

This morning started none too well, either.

Roy [*Hacker's driver, and like all drivers, one of the best-informed men in Whitehall – Ed.*] picked me up as usual, at about eight-thirty. I asked him to drive me to the Ministry, as I was to spend all morning on Health Service administration.

He started needling me right away.

'Chap just been talking about that on the radio,' he said casually. 'Saying the trouble with the health and education and transport services is that all the top people in government go to private hospitals and send their kids to private schools . . .'

I laughed it off, though I sounded a little mirthless, I fear. 'Very good. Comedy programme, was it?'

This egalitarian stuff, though daft, is always a little dangerous if it's not watched very carefully.

'And they go to work in chauffeur-driven cars,' added my chauffeur.

I didn't deign to reply. So he persisted.

'Don't you think there's something in it? I mean, if you and Sir Humphrey Appleby went to work on a number 27 . . .'

I interrupted him. 'Quite impractible,' I explained firmly. 'We work long enough hours as it is, without spending an extra hour a day waiting at the bus stop.'

'Yes,' said Roy. 'You'd have to make the bus service much more efficient, wouldn't you?'

'We certainly would,' I said, trying to dismiss the subject quickly.

'Yes,' said Roy. 'That's what he was saying, see?' The man should be a television interviewer.

'Same with the Health Service,' Roy continued inexorably. 'You a member of BUPA, sir?'

It was none of his bloody business. But I didn't say so. Instead, I smiled sweetly and asked if there was anything on the radio.

'*Yesterday in Parliament*, I think sir,' he replied, reaching for the switch.

'No, no, no, don't bother, don't bother,' I shrieked, casually, but too late. He switched it on, and I was forced to listen to myself.

Roy listened with great interest. After it got to Second Order he switched it off. There was a bit of an awkward silence.

'I got away with it, didn't I?' I asked hopefully.

Roy chuckled. 'You were lucky they didn't ask you about that new St Edward's Hospital,' he said jovially.

'Why?'

'Well . . .' he smacked his lips. 'They finished building it fifteen months ago – and it's still got no patients.'

'I suppose,' I said, 'the DHSS haven't got enough money to staff it.'

'Oh, it's got *staff*,' said Roy. 'Five hundred administrators. Just no patients.'

Could this be true? It hardly seemed possible.

'Who told you this?' I asked cautiously.

'The lip.'

'The lip?'

[*The slang word used by drivers to describe he who knows the most – Ed.*]

'My mate Charlie,' he explained. 'He knows all right. He's the driver for the Secretary of State for Health.'

When I got to the office I summoned Humphrey at once. I told him straight out that I was appalled by yesterday's debate.

'So am I, Minister,' Humphrey said. I was slightly surprised to find him agreeing so vehemently.

'The stupidity of it . . . the incompetence,' I continued.

'I agree,' said Humphrey. 'I can't think what came over you.'

I blinked at him. 'I beg your pardon?'

'To concede a full *independent* enquiry . . .'

So that was it. I stopped him dead in his tracks. 'Humphrey!' I said magisterially. 'That is not what I am talking about.'

Sir Humphrey looked puzzled. 'But you mentioned stupidity and incompetence.'

'Yours, Humphrey!' I roared. '*Yours!*'

Now it seemed to be his turn to be astounded. '*Mine*, Minister?' He was incredulous.

'Yes. Yours. How could you drop me in it like that?'

To be fair, he personally hadn't dropped me in it. But his precious Department had. Humphrey, however, seemed disinclined to apologise.

'A small omission from the brief. We can't foresee everything.' Then his face resumed an expression of pure horror. 'But to concede a full independent enquiry . . .'

I'd had enough of this. 'I didn't particularly want an enquiry either,' I pointed out. 'But if you're drowning and somebody throws you a rope, you grab it.'

'It was not a rope,' replied Sir Humphrey. 'It was a noose. You should have stood up for the Department – that is what you are here for.'

That may be what *Humphrey* thinks I'm here for. As a matter of fact, its nice to know he thinks I'm here for *something*. But I knew that if I didn't stop him he would give me a little lecture on Ministerial Responsibility.

The Doctrine of Ministerial Responsibility is a handy little device conceived by the Civil Service for dropping the Minister in it while enabling the mandarins to keep their noses clean. It means, in practice, that the Civil Service runs everything and takes all the decisions, but when something goes wrong then it's the Minister who takes the blame.

'No, Humphrey, it won't do,' I interjected firmly before he could go any further. 'I prepared myself thoroughly for Question Time yesterday. I mugged up all the Questions and literally dozens of supplementaries. I was up half Sunday night, I skipped lunch yesterday, I was thoroughly prepared.' I decided to say it again. '*Thoroughly*

17

prepared!' I said. 'But nowhere in my brief was there the slightest indication that you'd been juggling the figures so that I would be giving misleading replies to the House.'

'Minister,' said Humphrey in his most injured tones, 'you said you
wanted the administration figures reduced, didn't you?'

'Yes,' I agreed.

'So we reduced them.'

Dimly I began to perceive what he was saying. 'But . . . you only
reduced the *figures*, not the actual number of administrators!'

Sir Humphrey furrowed his brow. 'Of course.'

'Well,' I explained patiently, 'that was not what I meant.'

Sir Humphrey was pained. 'Well really Minister, we are not
mind-readers. You said reduce the figures, so we reduced the
figures.'

This was obvious nonsense. He knew perfectly well what I'd
meant, but had chosen to take my instructions literally. It was because of this sort of Civil Service foolishness and unhelpfulness that
this country is literally bleeding to death.

[*We assume that Hacker did not literally mean literally – Ed.*]

'How did it get out?' I demanded. 'Another leak. This isn't a
Department, it's a colander.' I was rather pleased with that little
crack. Sir Humphrey ignored it, of course. 'How can we govern re-
sponsibly,' I continued, 'if backbenchers are going to get all the
facts?' There was another silence. Naturally. There was no answer
to that one. 'Anyway,' I concluded, 'at least an enquiry gives us a little time.'

'So does a time bomb,' observed my Permanent Secretary.

So I waited to see if he had a disposal squad up his sleeve.
Apparently not.

'If only you'd said we'd have a Departmental Enquiry,' he complained, 'then we could have made it last eighteen months, and
finally said that it revealed a certain number of anomalies which
have now been rectified but that there was no evidence of any intention to mislead. Something like that.'

I allowed myself to be diverted for a moment. 'But there *was* an
intention to mislead,' I pointed out.

'I never said there wasn't,' Sir Humphrey replied impatiently. 'I
merely said there was no evidence of it.'

I think I was looking blank. He explained.

'The job of a professionally conducted internal enquiry is to un-
earth a grea. mass of no evidence. If you say there was no intention,

18

you can be proved wrong. But if you say the enquiry found no *evidence* of an intention, you can't be proved wrong.'

This is a most interesting insight into one of the Civil Service favourite devices. In future I'll know what is *really* meant by a departmental enquiry. Even a full departmental enquiry. That would presumably mean that an even greater mass of no evidence had been unearthed for the occasion.

However I had to deal with the matter in hand, namely that I had agreed to an independent enquiry. 'Couldn't we,' I suggested thoughtfully, 'get an independent enquiry to find no evidence?'

'You mean, rig it?' enquired Sir Humphrey coldly.

This man's double standards continue to amaze me.

'Well . . . yes!'

'Minister!' he said, as if he was deeply shocked. Bloody hypocrite. 'What's wrong with rigging an independent enquiry if you can rig an internal one, I should like to know?' Though I already know the answer – you might get *caught* rigging an independent enquiry.

'No, Minister, in an independent enquiry everything depends on who the Chairman is. He absolutely has to be sound.'

'If he's sound,' I remarked 'surely there's a danger he'll bring it all out into the open?'

Sir Humphrey was puzzled again. 'No, not if he's sound,' he explained. 'A sound man will understand what is required. He will perceive the implications. He will have a sensitive and sympathetic insight into the overall problem.'

He *was* suggesting that we rig it, in fact. He just likes to wrap it up a bit.

'Ah,' I said. 'So "sound" actually means "bent"?'

'Certainly not!' He was too quick with his denial. Methinks Sir Humphrey doth protest too much. 'I mean,' he tried again, 'a man of broad understanding . . .'

I decided to short circuit the process by making some suggestions.

'Then what about a retired politician?'

'. . . and unimpeachable integrity,' concluded Humphrey.

'Oh I see.' I paused to think. 'What about an academic or a businessman?'

Sir Humphrey shook his head.

'Okay,' I said, knowing that he had someone in mind already. 'Out with it. Who?'

'Well, Minister, I thought perhaps . . . a retired civil servant.'

I saw his point. 'Good thinking Humphrey.' It's wonderful what years of training can do for you!

'Sir Maurice Williams could be the man,' he went on.

I wasn't too sure about this. 'You don't think he might be too independent?'

'He's hoping for a peerage,' said Humphrey quietly, with a smile. He appeared to think he was producing an ace from up his sleeve.

I was surprised. 'This won't give him one, will it?'

'No, but the right finding will give him a few more Brownie points.'

Brownie points. This was a new concept to me. Humphrey explained that they all add up until you get the badge. This seems to make sense.

'Right,' I said decisively. 'Sir Maurice it is.' Thank God I find it so easy to take decisions.

'Thank you, Brown Owl,' smiled Humphrey, and left the room. He's really quite a pleasant fellow when he gets his way, and perhaps his idea will get us out of the embarrassment of an independent enquiry actually revealing anything – whether it be something we didn't know ourselves and should have known, or something we knew perfectly well and didn't want others to know we had known.

Of course, I realise on reflection that there is a third, and more real, possibility – that an independent enquiry would reveal something that Humphrey knew and I didn't know and that he didn't want me to know and that I would look an idiot for not knowing.

Like what happened yesterday, in other words.

So perhaps it's just as well to follow his advice, until the day dawns when I know some embarrassing information that he doesn't.

March 5th

A long meeting with Bernard Woolley today.

First of all, he was concerned about the Cuban refugees. Naturally. I'm concerned about them too. There's a whole row brewing in Parliament and the press about the government's refusal to help them.

I tried to point out that its not my fault the Treasury won't give us the cash.

I can't beat the Treasury. No one can beat the Treasury.

I've decided to do nothing about the refugees because there's nothing I can do. However, Bernard and I had a more fruitful and revealing conversation about the new St Edward's Hospital that Roy had tipped me off about yesterday. It seemed at first as though Roy was misinformed.

'You asked me to find out about that alleged empty hospital in North London,' began Bernard.

I nodded.

'Well, as I warned you, the driver's network is not wholly reliable. Roy has got it wrong.'

I was very relieved. 'How did you find out this good news?' I asked.

'Through the Private Secretaries' network.'

This was impressive. Although the Private Secretaries' network is sometimes a little slower than the drivers' network, it is a great deal more reliable – in fact almost 100% accurate.

'And?'

Bernard explained that at this hospital there are only 342 administrative staff. The other 170 are porters, cleaners, laundry workers, gardeners, cooks and so forth.

This seemed a perfectly reasonable figure. So I asked how many medical staff.

'Oh, none of *them*,' replied Bernard casually, as if that were perfectly obvious in any case.

I wasn't sure I'd heard right. 'None?' I asked, cautiously.

'None,' he agreed contentedly.

I decided to clarify a thing or two. 'We are talking about St Edward's *Hospital*, aren't we, Bernard?'

'Oh yes,' he answered cheerfully. 'It's brand new, you see,' he added as if that explained everything.

'How new?'

'Well,' he said, 'it was completed eight months ago, and fully staffed, but unfortunately there were government cutbacks at that time and there was, consequently, no money left for the medical services.'

My mind was slowly boggling. 'A brand new hospital,' I repeated quietly, to make sure I had not misheard, 'with five hundred medical staff and no patients?'

I sat and thought quietly for a few moments.

Then Bernard said helpfully, 'Well there is one patient, actually, Minister?'

'One?' I said.

'Yes – the Deputy Chief Administrator fell over a piece of scaffolding and broke his leg.'

I began to recover myself. 'My God,' I said. 'What if I'd been asked about this in the House?' Bernard looked sheepish. 'Why didn't I know? Why didn't you tell me?'

'I didn't know either.'

'Why didn't you know? Who *did* know? How come this hasn't got out?'

Bernard explained that apparently one or two people at the DHSS knew. And they have told him that this is not unusual – in fact, there are several such hospitals dotted around the country.

It seems there is a standard method of preventing this kind of thing leaking out. 'Apparently it has been contrived to keep it looking like a building site, and so far no one has realised that the hospital is operational. You know, scaffolding and skips and things still there. The normal thing.'

I was speechless. 'The normal thing?' I said. [*Apparently, not quite speechless – Ed.*]

'I think . . .' I was in my decisive mood again, '. . . I *think* I'd better go and see it for myself, before the Opposition get hold of this one.'

'Yes,' said Bernard. 'It's surprising that the press haven't found out by now, isn't it?'

I informed Bernard that most of our journalists are so amateur that they would have grave difficulty in finding out that today is Thursday.

'It's actually Wednesday, Minister,' he said.

I pointed to the door.

[*The following Tuesday Sir Humphrey Appleby met Sir Ian Whitchurch, Permanent Secretary of the Department of Health and Social Security, at the Reform Club in Pall Mall. They discussed St Edward's Hospital. Fortunately, Sir Humphrey made a note about this conversation on one of his special pieces of margin-shaped memo paper. Sir Humphrey preferred to write in margins where possible, but, if not possible, simulated margins made him feel perfectly comfortable – Ed.*]

Ian was understandably concerned about Hacker's sudden interest in St Edward's Hospital.

[*We can infer from this note that Mr Bernard Woolley – as he then was – mentioned the matter of St Edward's Hospital to Sir Humphrey, although when we challenged Sir Bernard – as he now is – on this point he had no recollection of doing so – Ed.*]

I explained that my Minister was greatly concerned that the hospital contained no patients.

We shared a certain sense of amusement on this point. My Minister was making himself faintly ridiculous. How can a hospital have patients when it has no nursing staff?

Ian quite rightly pointed out that they have great experience at the DHSS in getting hospitals going. The first step is to sort out the smooth-running of the place. Having patients around would be no help at all – they'd just get in the way. Ian therefore advised me to tell Hacker that this is the run-in period for St Edward's.

However, anticipating further misplaced disquiet in political circles, I pressed Ian for an answer to the question: How long is the run-in period going to run? I was forced to refer to my Minister's agreeing to a full independent enquiry.

Ian reiterated the sense of shock that he had felt on hearing of the independent enquiry. Indeed, I have no doubt that his shock is reflected throughout Whitehall.

Nevertheless, I was obliged to press him further. I asked for an indication that we are going to get some patients into St Edward's *eventually*.

Sir Ian said that if possible, we would. He confirmed that it is his present intention to have some patients at the hospital, probably in a couple of years when the financial situation has eased up.

This seems perfectly reasonable to me. I do not see how he can open forty new wards at St Edwards while making closures elsewhere. The Treasury wouldn't wear it, and nor would the Cabinet.

But knowing my Minister, he may not see things in the same light. He may, *simply* because the hospital is treating no patients, attempt to shut down the whole place.

I mentioned this possibility to Ian, who said that such an idea was quite impossible. The unions would prevent it.

It seemed to me that the unions might not yet be active at St Edward's, but Ian had an answer for that – he reminded me of Billy Fraser, the firebrand agitator at Southwark Hospital. Dreadful man. He could be useful.

Ian's going to move him on, I think. [*Appleby Papers 19/SPZ/116*]

[*Perhaps we should point out that Hacker would not have been informed of the conversation described above, and Sir Humphrey's memo was made purely as a private aide-memoire – Ed.*]

March 12th

Today I had a showdown with Humphrey over Health Service Administration.

I had a lot of research done for me at Central House [*Hacker's party headquarters – Ed.*] because I was unable to get clear statistics out of my own Department. Shocking!

They continually change the basis of comparative figures from year to year, thus making it impossible to check what kind of bureaucratic growth is going on.

'Humphrey,' I began, fully armed with chapter and verse, 'the whole National Health Service is an advanced case of galloping bureaucracy.'

Humphrey seemed unconcerned. 'Certainly not,' he replied. 'Not galloping. A gentle canter at the most.'

I told him that instances of idiotic bureaucracy flood in daily.

'From whom?'

'MPs,' I said. 'And constituents, and doctors and nurses. The public.'

Humphrey wasn't interested. 'Troublemakers,' he said.

I was astonished. 'The public?'

'They are some of the worst,' he remarked.

I decided to show him the results of some of my researches. First I showed him a memo about stethoscopes. [*As luck would have it, Hacker kept copies of all the memos to which he refers in his diary. These give us a fascinating insight into the running of the National Health Service in the 1980s – Ed.*]

Royal United Hospital

STETHOSCOPE REQUISITION

Because of the current supply situation
it is not possible to issue you with
the extra stethoscopes you have applied
for.

We are, however, in a position to supply
you with longer tubes for your existing
stethoscopes.

Purchasing Dept

Sir Humphrey saw nothing strange in this and commented that if a supply of longer tubes was available it was right and proper to make such an offer.

Bernard then went so far as to suggest that it could save a lot of wear and tear on the doctors – with sufficiently long tubes for their stethoscopes, he suggested, they could stand in one place and listen to all the chests on the ward.

I hope and pray that he was being facetious.

Then I showed Humphrey the memos from St Stephen's about toilet rolls and the mortuary.

From: The Chief Administrator

To: All Medical Staff

St Stephen's mortuary will be closed over Christmas. During the holiday medical staff are requested to co-operate in keeping pressure off this department.

From: Almoner

To: All Staff

Will you please note that soft paper toilet rolls are provided only for the use of patients, and not staff. It would appear that, in recent months, staff have been using the soft toilet rolls, for one reason or another.

Sir Humphrey brushed these memos aside. He argued that the Health Service is as efficient and economical as the government allows it to be.

So I showed him a quite remarkable document from the Director of Uniforms in a Regional Health Authority:

Regional Health Authority

NURSES' UNIFORMS

It has become apparent that the latest consignment of nurses coats are made of a see-through material.

Nurses who have been issued with these coats are requested to report to the Director of the Uniform Surveillance Centre, who will assess the nature of the problem.

Director of Uniforms

Humphrey had the grace to admit he was amazed by this piece of nonsense. 'Nice work if you can get it,' he said with a smile.

I saved my trump card till last. And even Humphrey was concerned about the Christmas dinner memo:

FLORENCE NIGHTINGALE INFIRMARY

KITCHEN RE-ORGANISATION   December 13

Festive arrangements

Please note that Tuesday's sweet will be served as first course on Friday and Friday's first course will be served as main course on Thursday. The Christmas Dinner will be served on New Year's Eve and the New Year's Party will take place on Boxing Day. That, of course, means that staff will have to bring their own lunch on January 7th.

Good Friday this year will be held on Tuesday April 14th.

Chief of Catering

Humphrey did at least admit that something might be slightly wrong if we are paying people throughout the NHS to toil away at producing all this meaningless drivel. And I learned this morning that in ten years the number of Health Service administrators has gone up by 40,000 and the number of hospital beds has gone down by 60,000. These figures speak for themselves.

Furthermore the annual cost of the Health Service has gone up by one and a half billion pounds. In real terms!

But Sir Humphrey seemed pleased when I gave him these figures. 'Ah,' he said smugly, 'if only British industry could match this growth record.'

I was staggered! 'Growth?' I said. 'Growth,' I repeated. Were my ears deceiving me? 'Growth?' I cried. He nodded. 'Are you suggesting that treating fewer and fewer patients so that we can employ more and more administrators is a proper use of the funds voted by Parliament and supplied by the taxpayer?'

'Certainly.' He nodded again.

I tried to explain to him that the money is only voted to make sick people better. To my intense surprise, he flatly disagreed with this proposition.

'On the contrary, Minister, it makes *everyone* better – better for having shown the extent of their care and compassion. When money is allocated to Health and Social Services, Parliament and the country feel cleansed. Absolved. Purified. It is a sacrifice.'

This, of course, was pure sophism. 'The money should be spent on patient care, surely?'

Sir Humphrey clearly regarded my comment as irrelevant. He pursued his idiotic analogy. 'When a sacrifice has been made, nobody asks the Priest what happened to the ritual offering after the ceremony.'

Humphrey is wrong, wrong, wrong, wrong! In my view the country *does* care if the money is mis-spent, and I'm there as the country's representative, to see that it isn't.

'With respect,[1] Minister,' began Humphrey, one of his favourite insults in his varied repertoire, 'people merely care that the money is not *seen* to be mis-spent.'

I rejected that argument. I reminded him of the uproar over the mental hospital scandals.

Cynical as ever, he claimed that such an uproar proved his point. 'Those abuses had been going on quite happily for decades,' he said. 'No one was remotely concerned to find out what was being done with their money – it was their sacrifice, in fact. What outraged them was being told about it.'

I realised that this whole ingenious theory, whether true or false, was being used by Humphrey as a smokescreen. I decided to ask a straight question.

'Are we or aren't we agreed that there is no point in keeping a hospital running for the benefit of the staff?'

[1] Meaning without respect.

Humphrey did not give a straight answer.

'Minister,' he admonished, 'that is not how I would have expressed the question.'

Then he fell silent.

I pointed out that that was how I had expressed it.

'Indeed,' he said.

And waited.

Clearly, he had no intention of answering any straight question unless it was expressed in terms which he found wholly acceptable.

I gave in. 'All right,' I snapped, 'how would you express it?'

'At the end of the day,' he began, '*one* of a hospital's prime functions is patient care.'

'One?' I said. 'One? What else?'

He refused to admit that I had interrupted him, and continued speaking with utter calm as if I had not said a word. 'But, until we have the money for the nursing and medical staff, that is a function that we are not able to pursue. Perhaps in eighteen months or so . . .'

'Eighteen months?' I was appalled.

'Yes, perhaps by then we may be able to open a couple of wards,' he said, acknowledging finally that I had spoken.

I regard this as so much stuff and nonsense. I instructed him to open some wards at once – and more than a couple.

He countered by offering to form an inter-departmental committee to examine the feasibility of monitoring a proposal for admitting patients at an earlier date.

I asked him how long that would take to report.

'Not long, Minister.'

'How long?'

I knew the answer before he gave it – 'Eighteen months,' we said in unison.

'Terrific!' I added sarcastically.

'Thank you,' he replied, charmingly unaware. It's hopeless.

So I made a new suggestion. 'I suggest that we get rid of everyone currently employed at the hospital and use the money to open closed wards in other hospitals.'

[*As Sir Humphrey had predicted, Hacker was prepared to shut down the whole hospital – Ed.*]

'And when we can afford it,' I added sarcastically, 'we'll open St Edwards with *medical staff!* If you would be so kind.'

Humphrey then argued that if we closed the hospital now we

would delay the opening of it *with patients* for years. 'You talk,' he said accusingly, 'as if the staff have nothing to do, simply because there are no patients there.'

'What *do* they do?' I asked.

Humphrey was obviously expecting this question. He promptly handed me a list. A list comprising all the administrative departments and what they do – with or without patients. Extraordinary.

St. Edwards Hospital

DEPARTMENTAL LIST

Effective January 1st

The purpose of this Departmental List is to facilitate liaison between Departments.

ISSUED BY PERSONNEL SERVICES

1   Contingency Planning Department

For strikes, air raids, nuclear war, fire epidemics, food or water poisoning, etc. In such a crisis your local general hospital will become a key centre for survival.

2   Data and Research Department

Currently this department is conducting a full-scale demographic survey of the catchment area. This is to enable the hospital to anticipate future requirements for maternity, paediatrics, geriatrics and the male/female balance.

3   Finance

Projected accounts, balance sheets, cash flow estimates depending on such variables as admission levels, inflation rate, local and national level.

4   Purchasing Department

To purchase medical and other supplies, obtain estimates, review current and future catalogues and price lists.

5   Technical Department

For evaluating all proposed equipment purchases and comparing cost-effectiveness.

1.   *Contingency Planning Department*
For strikes, air raids, nuclear war, fire epidemics, food or water poisoning, etc. In such a crisis your local general hospital will become a key centre for survival.

2.   *Data And Research Department*
Currently this department is conducting a full-scale demographic survey of the catchment area. This is to enable the hospital to anticipate future requirements for maternity, paediatrics, geriatrics and the male/female balance.

3. *Finance*
Projected accounts, balance sheets, cash flow estimates depending on such variables as admission levels, inflation rate, local and national funding etc.

4. *Purchasing Department*
To purchase medical and other supplies, obtain estimates, review current and future catalogues and price lists.

5. *Technical Department*
For evaluating all proposed equipment purchases and comparing cost-effectiveness.

6. *Building Department*
To deal with the Phase Three building plans, the costing, the architectural liaison, and all other work necessary to complete the final phase of the hospital by 1994.

7. *Maintenance*
Maintenance of both the hospital structure itself, and the highly complex and expensive medical and technical equipment contained therein.
As an economy measure, this department also includes the Cleaning Department.

8. *Catering*
This department is self-explanatory.

9. *Personnel*
A very busy department, dealing with leave, National Health Insurance, and salaries. Naturally this department contains a number of staff welfare officers, who are needed to look after over 500 employees.

10. *Administration*
The typing pool, desks, stationery, office furniture and equipment, liaison between departments, agreeing on routine procedures.

    I couldn't tell as I read this (and tonight I still can't) if Humphrey was playing a practical joke. Department 10 contains administrators to administrate other administrators.

    I read it carefully, then I studied his face. He appeared to be serious.

    'Humphrey,' I said, very slowly and carefully. 'There-are-no-patients! That-is-what-a-hospital-is-for! Patients! Ill-people! Heal-ing-the-sick!'

    Sir Humphrey was unmoved. 'I agree, Minister,' he said, 'but nonetheless all of these vital tasks that I have listed here must be carried on with or without patients.'

    'Why?' I asked.

    He looked blank. 'Why?'

'Yes. Why?' I repeated.

'I don't understand,' he said.

I tried to rack my brains, to see how else I could put it. I finally gave up.

'Why?' I asked.

'Minister,' he said, 'would you get rid of the Army just because there's no war?'

A completely specious argument, and I told him so. He asked me how I would define specious. I dodged the question, and hurriedly pointed out that hospitals are different. Hospital must get results!

At last I appeared to have shocked him. He was completely shaken out of his complacency.

'Minister,' he said earnestly, 'we don't measure our success by results, but by activity. And the activity is considerable. And productive. These 500 people are seriously overworked – the full establishment should be 650.' He opened his briefcase. 'May I show you some of the paperwork emanating from St Edward's Hospital?'

That was the *last* thing I wanted to see.

'No you may not,' I replied firmly. 'Enough is enough. Sack them all.'

He refused point blank. He said it was impossible. He repeated that if we lost our administrators the hospital would *never* open. So I told him just to sack the ancillary workers. He said the unions wouldn't wear it.

I compromised. I instructed him to sack half the administrators and half the ancillary workers. I told him to replace them with medical staff and open a couple of wards. I also told him that it was my last word on the subject.

He tried to keep the discussion going. I wouldn't let him. But he seemed worryingly complacent about the whole situation, and as he left he said he would have a word with the Health Service unions. He held out little hope that such a solution were possible.

I'm beginning to feel like Alice in Wonderland.

[*Later that week Sir Humphrey Appleby had a meeting with Brian Baker, the General Secretary of the Confederation of Administrative Unions. It seems to have taken place privately, over a glass of sherry, after another meeting in Sir Humphrey's office. Most unusually, Sir Humphrey appears to have made no notes, memos or references to the meeting, not even in his private diary. This suggests that he regarded the discussion as potentially highly embarrassing. Fortunately, however, Brian Baker referred to this secret discussion at the*

next meeting of his Union's National Executive, and his account of it
appears in the minutes – Ed.]

Confederation of Administrative Unions

Any Other Business:

Mr Baker reported a highly confidential meeting to the Executive Committee. He
had had a talk with Sir Humphrey Appleby, Permanent Secretary of the DAA, which
they had both agreed should remain completely confidential and just between
themselves. Sir Humphrey had raised the matter of St Edward's Hospital. Mr
Baker had indicated that he was prepared to take a soft line in these negotiations;
he felt that we had not much of a case. It could be hard to argue that the
government should keep ancillary staff on indefinitely in an empty hospital.

Sir Humphrey accused Mr Baker of defeatism, and ordered him to stick up for his
members. Mr Baker reported that he was initially surprised by this suggestion,
until Sir Humphrey pointed out that the 342 administrators must have some workers
to administer - or they too would be on the dole.

Mr Baker was surprised at this indication that Sir Humphrey might be forced to
lay off some Civil Servants. But as Sir Humphrey had said to him "we live now
in strange and disturbing times".

Any Other Business:
Mr Baker reported a highly confidential meeting to the Executive Committee. He had had a talk with Sir Humphrey Appleby, Permanent Secretary
of the DAA, which they had both agreed would remain completely confidential and just between themselves.

Sir Humphrey had raised the matter of St Edward's Hospital. Mr Baker
had indicated that he was prepared to take a soft line in these negotiations;
he felt that we had not much of a case. It could be hard to argue that the
government should keep ancillary staff on indefinitely in an empty hospital.

Sir Humphrey accused Mr Baker of defeatism, and ordered him to stick
up for his members. Mr Baker reported that he was initially surprised by
this suggestion, until Sir Humphrey pointed out that the 342 administrators
must have some workers to administer – or they too would be on the dole.

Mr Baker was surprised at this indication that Sir Humphrey might be
forced to lay off some civil servants. But as Sir Humphrey had said to him
'we live now in strange and disturbing times.'

Mr Baker asked if Sir Humphrey would support the union if we took industrial action. Sir Humphrey pointed out that he is charged with keeping
the wheels of government in motion, and could not possibly countenance a
show of solidarity.

Nevertheless, he hinted that he would not come down heavy on a wide-
spread and effective show of opposition from our members.

Mr Baker wanted to know where the Minister stood on this matter. Sir
Humphrey explained that the Minister does not know his ACAS from his
NALGO.

Mr Baker then indicated that, if he was to cause effective disruption, he needed some active help and support from Sir Humphrey. What with the hospital empty for fifteen months and no hope of opening any wards for another year or more, he informed Sir Humphrey that our members were resigned and apathetic.

Sir Humphrey asked if Billy Fraser was resigned or apathetic. At first Mr Baker thought Sir Humphrey did not realise that Fraser is at Southwark Hospital. But Sir Humphrey indicated that he could soon be transferred to St Edward's.

The Assistant General Secretary commented that this is good news. We can do much to improve our members pay and conditions at St Edwards if there is some real shop floor militancy to build on.

Finally, Mr Baker reported that Sir Humphrey escorted him out of the door, offering good wishes to his fraternal comrades and singing 'we shall overcome'.

The Executive Commitee urged Mr Baker to keep a close eye on Sir Humphrey Appleby in all future negotiations because of the possibility either that he's a traitor to his class or that he's going round the twist.

Brian Baker, General Secretary of the Confederation of Administrative Unions relaxing after a successful meeting of his National Executive Committee (Reproduced by kind permission of his grandson)

March 17th
[Hacker's diary continues – Ed.]
Today I paid an official visit to St Edward's Hospital. It was a real eye-opener.

The Welcoming Committee – I use the term in the very broadest sense, because I can hardly imagine a group of people who were less welcoming – were lined up on the steps.

I met Mrs Rogers, the Chief Administrator, and an appalling

Glaswegian called Billy Fraser who rejoices in the title of Chairman of the Joint Shop Stewards Negotiating Committee. Mrs Rogers was about forty-five. Very slim, dark hair with a grey streak – a very handsome Hampstead lady who speaks with marbles in the mouth.

'How very nice to meet you,' I said, offering to shake his hand.

'I wouldn't count on it,' he snarled.

I was shown several empty wards, several administrative offices that were veritable hives of activity, and finally a huge deserted dusty operating theatre suite.

I enquired about the cost of the suite. Mrs Rogers informed me that, together with Radiotherapy and Intensive Care, it cost two and a quarter million pounds.

I asked her if she was not horrified that the place was not in use.

'No,' she said cheerfully. 'Very good thing in some ways. Prolongs its life. Cuts down running costs.'

'But there are no patients,' I reminded her.

She agreed. 'Nonetheless,' she added, 'the essential work of the hospital has to go on.'

'I thought the patients were the essential work of the hospital.'

'Running an organisation of five hundred people is a big job, Minister,' said Mrs Rogers, beginning to sound impatient with me.

'Yes,' I spluttered, 'but if they weren't here they wouldn't be here.'

'What?'

Obviously she wasn't getting my drift. She has a completely closed mind.

I decided that it was time to be decisive. I told her that this situation could not continue. Either she got patients into the hospital, or I closed it.

She started wittering. 'Yes, well, Minister, in the course of time I'm sure . . .'

'Not in the course of time,' I said. '*Now*. We will get rid of three hundred of your people and use the savings to pay for some doctors and nurses so that we can get some patients in.'

Billy Fraser then started to put in his two pen'orth.

'Look here,' he began, 'without those two hundred people this hospital just wouldn't function.'

'Do you think its functioning now?' I enquired.

Mrs Rogers was unshakeable in her self-righteousness. 'It is one of the best-run hospitals in the country,' she said. 'It's up for the Florence Nightingale award.'

I asked what that was, pray.

'It's won,' she told me proudly, 'by the most hygenic hospital in the Region.'

I asked God silently to give me strength. Then I told her that I'd said my last word and that three hundred staff must go, doctors and nurses hired, and patients admitted.

'You mean, three hundred jobs lost?' Billy Fraser's razor sharp brain had finally got the point.

Mrs Rogers had already got the point. But Mrs Rogers clearly felt that this hospital had no need of patients. She said that in any case they couldn't do any serious surgery with just a skeleton medical staff. I told her that I didn't care whether or not she did serious surgery – she could do nothing but varicose veins, hernias and piles for all I cared. But *something* must be done.

'Do you mean three hundred jobs lost,' said Billy Fraser angrily, still apparently seeking elucidation of the simple point everybody else had grasped ten minutes ago.

I spelt it out to him. 'Yes I do, Mr Fraser,' I replied. 'A hospital is not a source of employment, it is a place to heal the sick.'

He was livid. His horrible wispy beard was covered in spittle as he started to shout abuse at me, his little pink eyes blazing with class hatred and alcohol. 'It's a source of employment for my members,' he yelled. 'You want to put them out of work, do you, you bastard?' he screamed. 'Is that what you call a compassionate society?'

I was proud of myself. I stayed calm. 'Yes,' I answered coolly. 'I'd rather be compassionate to the patients than to your members.'

'We'll come out on strike,' he yelled.

I couldn't believe my eyes or ears. I was utterly delighted with that threat. I laughed in his face.

'Fine,' I said happily. 'Do that. What does it matter? Who can you harm? Please, do go on strike, the sooner the better. And take all those administrators with you,' I added, waving in the direction of the good Mrs Rogers. 'Then we won't have to pay you.'

Bernard and I left the battlefield or St Edward's Hospital, I felt, as the undisputed victors of the day.

It's very rare in politics that one has the pleasure of completely wiping the floor with one's opponents. It's a good feeling.

March 18th
Bad news today. The whole picture changed in a most surprising fashion.

Bernard and I were sitting in the office late this afternoon congratulating ourselves on yesterday's successes. I was saying, rather smugly I fear, that Billy Fraser's strike threat had played right into my hands.

We turned on the television news. First there was an item saying that the British Government is again being pressured by the US Government to take some more Cuban refugees. And then – the bombshell! Billy Fraser came on, and threatened that the whole of the NHS in London would be going on strike on Friday midnight if we laid off workers at St Edwards. I was shattered.

[*We have been fortunate to obtain the transcript of the television news programme in question, and it is reproduced below – Ed.*]

BRITISH BROADCASTING CORPORATION

NEWSREADER: All workers in National Health Service hospitals in the Greater London area are to go on strike at Friday midnight. A row has blown up at St Edward's Hospital over the proposed laying off of one hundred and seventy ancillary workers. We spoke to Union activist Billy Fraser.

CUE TELECINE:

BILLY FRASER: We're striking against unemployment. We will bring London's hospitals literally to their knees. There will be a complete standstill: no blood transfusions, no operations, no cancer treatment, nothing! Not until we have brought back the compassionate society.

REPORTER: But how can you do this to the patients?

BILLY FRASER: We're not doing it. It's Mr Hacker that's doing it.

REPORTER: Shouldn't you think twice before inflicting these terrible sanctions on innocent members of the public?

BILLY FRASER: I can assure you, and I'd like to take this opportunity to assure the general public that every stone will be left unturned in the search for a settlement.

Humphrey came in at that moment.

'Oh,' he said, 'you're watching it.'

'Yes,' I said through clenched teeth. 'Humphrey, you told me you were going to have a word with the unions.'

'I did,' he replied. 'But well, what can I do?' He shrugged helplessly. I'm sure he did his best with the unions. But where has it got us?

I asked him what we were supposed to do now.

But Humphrey had come, apparently, on a different matter – of equal urgency. Another bombshell, in fact!

'It looks as if Sir Maurice Williams' independent enquiry is going to be unfavourable to us,' he began.

I was appalled. Humphrey had promised me that Williams was sound. He had told me that the man wanted a peerage.

'Unfortunately,' murmured Sir Humphrey, embarrassed, looking at his shoes, 'he's also trying to work his peerage in his capacity as Chairman of the Joint Committee for the Resettlement of Refugees.'

I enquired if there were more Brownie points in refugees than in government enquiries.

He nodded.

I pointed out that we simply haven't got the money to house any more refugees.

Then came bombshell number three! The phone rang. It was Number Ten.

I got on the line. I was told rather sharply by a senior policy advisor that Number Ten had seen Billy Fraser on the six o'clock news. By 'Number Ten' he meant the PM. Number Ten hoped a peace formula could be found very soon.

As I was contemplating this euphemistic but heavy threat from Downing Street, Humphrey was still rattling on about the boring old Cuban refugees. Sir Maurice would be satisfied if we just housed a thousand of them, he said.

As I was about to explain, yet again, that we haven't the time or the money to open a thousand bed hostel . . . the penny dropped!

A most beautiful solution had occurred to me.

A thousand refugees with nowhere to go. A thousand bed hospital, fully staffed. Luck was on our side after all. The symmetry was indescribably lovely.

Humphrey saw what I was thinking, of course, and seemed all set to resist. 'Minister,' he began, 'that hospital has millions of pounds of high technology equipment. It was built for sick British, not healthy foreigners. There is a huge Health Service waiting list. It would be an act of the most appalling financial irresponsibility to waste all that investment on . . .'

I interrupted this flow of hypocritical jingoistic nonsense.

'But . . .' I said carefully, 'what about the independent enquiry? Into our department? Didn't you say that Sir Maurice's enquiry was going to come down against us? Is that what you want?'

He paused. 'I see your point, Minister,' he replied thoughtfully.

I told Bernard to reinstate, immediately, all the staff at St Edward's, to tell Sir Maurice we are making a brand-new hospital available to accommodate a thousand refugees, and to tell the press it was my decision. Everyone was going to be happy!

Bernard asked me for a quote for the press release. A good notion.

'Tell them,' I said, 'that Mr Hacker said that this was a tough decision but a necessary one, if we in Britain aim to be worthy of the name of . . . the compassionate society.'

I asked Humphrey if he was agreeable to all this.

'Yes Minister,' he said. And I thought I detected a touch of admiration in his tone.

2

Doing the
Honours

March 18th

I had a very unsatisfactory meeting today, with assorted secretaries
– Deputy Secretaries, Under Secretaries, and Assistant Secretaries.

I asked about economies in accommodation, in stationery acquisition, in parks and forestry commission administration, in data processing equipment, in the further education budget.

As always I was met with the usual vague and regretful murmurs
of 'No Minister,' 'Afraid not Minister,' 'Doesn't seem possible
Minister,' 'Sadly it cannot be, Minister,' 'We have done the utmost
possible, Minister,' 'Pared to the bone, Minister alas!' and so forth.

I reflected aloud that at least the Universities are not going to
cost us quite so much, now that overseas students are to pay fees
that cover the full cost of their education here.

'Unless,' someone said, 'you make the exceptions which have
been proposed to you.'

Nobody else at the meeting had been prepared to make exceptions. I couldn't see why I should. I remarked that as it seemed the
only available saving at the moment we had no choice but to hang
on to it.

As the meeting broke up Bernard reminded me again that the
Honours Secretary at Number Ten had been asking if I had
approved our Department's recommendations for the Honours List.

Curiously this was about the eighth time Bernard had asked me. I
enquired sarcastically if honours were really the most important
subject in the whole of the DAA.

Bernard replied, without any apparent awareness of my sarcasm,
that they were indeed the most important subject for the people on
the list. 'They're never off the phone,' he said pathetically. 'Some of
them don't seem to have slept for about three nights.'

I was mildly surprised. I thought it was all a formality. 'Ministers never veto Civil Service honours, do they?' I asked.

'Hardly ever. But it's theoretically possible. And they're all getting worried by the delay.'

I suddenly realised that Bernard had just told me that people *knew* they were on the list. How? The file is marked *strictly confidential.*

He shook his head sadly at me when I mentioned it. 'Oh Minister,' he replied, and smiled at me in a kindly fashion.

I was amused and embarrassed at my naïvité. But all that energy that goes into worrying about honours . . . If only they'd put a quarter of it into cutting expenditure. I asked Bernard how I could get this Department to want economies in the way they wanted OBEs and KCBs and so on.

A gleam came into Bernard's eye. 'Well,' he said, with a slightly mischievous air that I'd never noticed before. 'I've been thinking . . .' Then he hesitated.

'Go on.'

'No, no, no.'

'What was it?'

'No. Nothing, Minister.'

I was on tenterhooks. I knew he had something up his sleeve. 'Come on Bernard,' I ordered, 'spit it out.' Bernard did not spit it out. Instead, he tentatively explained that it was not his place, and he wouldn't suggest this, and he couldn't *possibly* recommend it, but . . . 'well . . . suppose you were to refuse to recommend any honours for Civil Servants who haven't cut their budgets by five per cent per annum?'

'Bernard!'

He retreated immediately.

'Oh, I'm so sorry, do forgive me Minister, I knew I shouldn't have . . .'

'No, no,' I said, hastily reassuring him. Bernard has great ideas but he needs much more confidence. 'It's brilliant!'

And indeed it is a brilliant idea. I was cock-a-hoop. It's our only hold over the civil servants. Ministers can't stop their pay rises, or their promotion. Ministers don't write their reports. Ministers have no real disciplinary authority. But Bernard is right – I can withhold honours! It's brilliant!

I congratulated him and thanked him profusely.

'You thought of it Minister!'

I didn't get the point at first. 'No, you did,' I told him generously.

'No, *you* did,' he said meaningfully. *'Please!'*

I understood. I nodded, and smiled reassuringly.

He looked even more anxious.

[*Some days later Sir Humphrey Appleby was invited to dine at the High Table of his alma mater, Baillie College, Oxford. He refers to the dinner and subsequent discussion in his private diary – Ed.*]

Had an excellent high table dinner at Baillie, followed by a private chat over the port and walnuts, with the Master and the Bursar. Clearly they were worried about the cuts.

Sir William [*Sir William Guthrie, the Master – Ed.*] was looking some-what the worse for wear – and the worse for the port. His hair is now quite white but his eyes were still the same clear penetrating blue.

Christopher [*Christopher Venables, the Bursar – Ed.*] still looked like the precise ex-RAF officer that he had been in the days before he became a don – tall, neat, and meticulous in manner and speech.

I asked the Master how he was feeling. He replied that he was feeling very old. But he smiled. 'I'm already an anomaly, I shall soon be an anachronism, and I have every intention of dying an abuse.' Very droll!

Guthrie and Venables started out by telling me that they intended to sell the rest of the rather delicious 1927 Fonseca[1] which we were drinking. Bail-lie has a couple of pipes left and the Bursar told me they'd fetch quite a bit. I couldn't think what they were talking about. I was astounded. Excellent shock tactics, of course. Then they told me that if they sold all the paintings and the silver, they could possibly pay off the entire mortgage on the new buildings.

They think – or want me to think – that Baillie College is going to the wall.

It transpired that the trouble is the government's policy of charging over-seas students the full economic rate for their tuition. Baillie has always had an exceptional number of overseas students.

The Bursar tells me that they cannot charge the full economic fee. £4000 per annum. Hardly anyone will pay it.

He says he has been everywhere! All over the USA, raising funds, trying to sell the idea of an Oxford education to the inhabitants of Podunk, Indi-ana, and Cedar Rapids, Wisconsin.

But the competition is cut-throat. Apparently Africa is simply crawling with British Professors frantically trying to flog sociology courses to the natives. And India. And the Middle East.

I suggested that they do the obvious thing – fill up the vacancies with British students.

This idea met with a very cold response. 'I don't think that's awfully funny, Humphrey,' the Master said.

He explained that home students were to be avoided at all costs! *Any-thing* but home students!

[1] Vintage port.

The reason is simple economics. Baillie only gets £500 per head for the UK students. Therefore, it would have to take four hundred home students to replace a mere fifty foreigners. The number of students at a tutorial would quadruple. The staff/student ratio would go from one in ten to one in thirty-four.

I see their point. Is this the end of civilisation as we know it? It would certainly be the end of Baillie College as we know it. There would be dormitories. Classrooms. It would be indistinguishable from Wormwood Scrubs or the University of Sussex.

And Hacker is the Minister who has the authority to change it. I had not realised the implications of all this, it being a DES decision. [*Department of Education and Science – Ed.*] Ours not to reason why, ours just to put the administrative wheels in motion.[1]

I suggested that we must persuade Hacker of the special and unique importance of Baillie College. He should be invited to dinner at High Table and the case explained to him.

The Master was noticeably worried about Hacker – he was concerned whether he was of the intellectual calibre to understand the case.

I pointed out that the case is intelligible to anyone of the intellectual calibre of Winnie-the-Pooh.

They asked me if Hacker *is* of the intellectual calibre of Winnie-the-Pooh. Clearly they've had dealings with politicians before.

I was able to reassure them on that point. I'm *fairly* sure that he is of the intellectual calibre of Winnie-the-Pooh. On his day.

[*Although Sir Humphrey, and Jim Hacker, were responsible for the implementation of these cuts, characteristically the Department of Education and Science had made them without consulting any of the other interested departments – the Foreign Office, or the Department of Health and Social Security or the Department of Administrative Affairs – Ed.*]

I left Oxford convinced that I must find a way to get Baillie recognised as a special institution (like Imperial College) for the extraordinary work that they do. [*A well-chosen adjective! As this episode in Hacker's life is fundamentally concerned with honours – deserved or undeserved, earned or unearned – we felt that at this point it might be of interest to the reader to know the principal honours conferred on the antagonists:*
Sir William Guthrie, OM, FRS, FBA, Ph.D, MC
Group Captain Christopher Venables, DSC, MA
Sir Humphrey Appleby, KCB, MVO, MA (Oxon)
Bernard Woolley, MA (Cantab)
The Rt Hon. James Hacker, PC, MP, BSc. (Econ)
Sir Arnold Robinson, GCMG, CVO, MA (Oxon) – Ed.]

---

[1] In fact, the size of Oxford University is limited by the University Grants Committee. Baillie might not even have been allowed to take more home students, except by taking them from other colleges. The other colleges would be unlikely to agree to this, because it would put them in jeopardy.

March 21st

This morning Humphrey badgered me again.

'Two things,' he said. 'First, there is the matter of the Departmental recommendations for the Honours List.'

I told him we'd leave that on one side for a bit.

He became very tense and twitchy. I tried not to show amusement. He told me we can't leave it as we are getting dangerously close to the five weeks.

[*All recipients of honours are notified at least five weeks before promulgation. Theoretically it gives them time to refuse. This is rare. In fact, the only time a civil servant is known to have refused a knighthood was in 1496. This was because he already had one – Ed.*]

I decided that I would not yet give my approval to the Department's Honours List, because I've been doing some research. [*Hacker almost certainly meant that a Party research assistant had been doing some research and he had read the report – Ed.*]

Incredibly, twenty per cent of all honours go to civil servants. The rest of the population of this country have to do something extra to get an honour. Over and above their ordinary work, for which they get paid. You or I have to do something special, like work with mentally-handicapped children for twenty-seven years, six nights a week – then we might get an MBE. But Civil Service knighthoods just come up with the rations.

These honours are, in any case, intrinsically ridiculous – MBE for instance, according to Whittaker's Almanack, stands for Member of the Most Honourable Order of the British Empire. Hasn't anyone in Whitehall noticed that we've lost the Empire?

The civil servants have been having it both ways for years. When Attlee was PM he got £5000 a year and the Cabinet Secretary got £2500. Now the Cabinet Secretary gets more than the PM. Why? Because civil servants used to receive honours as a compensation for long years of loyal public service, for which they got poor salaries, poor pension and few perks.

Now they have salaries comparable to executives in the most successful private enterprise companies (guess who's in charge of the comparability studies), inflation proof pensions, chauffeur-driven cars – and they *still* get automatic honours.

[*Hacker was right. The civil servants were undoubtedly manipulating the honours system to their own advantage. Just as incomes policies have always been manipulated by those that control them: for instance, the 1975 Pay Policy provided exemptions for Civil Service increments and lawyers' fees. Needless to say, the policy was drafted by civil servants and parliamentary draftsmen, i.e. lawyers.*

The problem is, quis custodiet ipsos custodes?[1] *– Ed.*]

So how can civil servants possibly understand the way the rest of us live, if they are immune to the basic threats to economic well-being faced by the rest of us: inflation and unemployment?

And how did the civil servants get away with creating these re-markably favourable terms of service for themselves? Simply by keeping a low profile. They have somehow managed to make people feel that discussing the matter at all is in rather poor taste.

But that cuts no ice with me. I believe in action now!

I asked Humphrey how he accounted for twenty per cent of hon-ours going to the Civil Service.

'A fitting tribute to their devotion to duty,' he said.

It's a pretty nice duty to be devoted to, I thought.

Humphrey continued: 'Her Majesty's civil servants spend their lives working for a modest wage and at the end they retire into obscurity. Honours are a small recompense for a lifetime of loyal, self-effacing discretion and devoted service to Her Majesty and to the nation.'

A pretty speech. But quite ridiculous. 'A modest wage?' I queried.

'Alas, yes.'

I explained to Humphrey, since he appeared to have forgotten, that he earned well over thirty thousand a year. Seven and a half thousand more than me.

He agreed, but insisted that it was still a relatively modest wage.

'Relative to whom?' I asked.

He was stuck for a moment. 'Well . . . Elizabeth Taylor for in-stance,' he suggested.

I felt obliged to explain to Sir Humphrey that he was in no way re-lative to Elizabeth Taylor. There are important differences.

'Indeed,' he agreed. 'She did not get a First in Greats.'[2]

Then, undaunted and ever persistent, he again asked me if I had approved the list. I made my move.

'No Humphrey,' I replied pleasantly, 'I am not approving any honour for anyone in this department who hasn't earned it.'

---

[1] Translation: who guards the guards? A quotation from Juvenal's *Satires* and not, as is commonly supposed in political circles, from juvenile satires.

[2] The Oxford term for the second part of the classics degree course.

Humphrey's face was a wonderful study in blankness.

'What do you mean, *earned* it?'

I explained that I meant earned it. In other words, having done something to deserve it.

The penny dropped. He exploded. 'But that's *unheard* of,' he exclaimed.

I smiled serenely. 'Maybe so. But my new policy is to stop all honours for all civil servants who fail to cut their department's budgets by five per cent a year.'

Humphrey was speechless.

So after a few moments I said: 'May I take it that your silence indicates approval?'

He found his voice fast. 'You may not, Minister.' He was deeply indignant. 'Where did you get this preposterous idea?'

I glanced at Bernard, who studied his right shoe lace intently. 'It came to me,' I said.

Humphrey was spluttering incoherently. 'It's ridiculous. It's out of the question. It's unthinkable.' Now that Humphrey had found his voice there was no stopping him. 'The whole idea . . . strikes at the whole root of . . . this is the beginning of the end . . . the thin end of the wedge . . . Bennite solution. [*Perhaps it was the word 'wedge' that reminded him of Benn – Ed.*] Where will it end? The abolition of the monarchy?'

I told him not to be silly. This infuriated him even more.

'There is *no reason*,' he said, stabbing the air with his finger, 'to change a system which has worked well in the past.'

'But it hasn't,' I said.

'We have to give the present system a fair trial,' he stated. This seems quite unremarkable on the face of it. But I reminded him that the Most Noble Order of the Garter was founded in 1348 by King Edward III. 'Surely it must be getting towards the end of its trial period?' I said.

So Humphrey tried a new tack. He said that to block honours pending economies might create a dangerous precedent.

What he means by 'dangerous precedent' is that if we do the right thing now, then we might be forced to do the right thing again next time. And on that reasoning nothing should ever be done at all. [*To be precise: many things may be done, but nothing must ever be done for the first time – Ed.*]

I told him I wasn't going to budge on my proposal. He resorted to barefaced lies, telling me that he was fully seized of my aims and had taken them on board and would do his best to put them into practice.

So I asked him point blank if he would put my policy into practice. He made me his usual offer. I know it off by heart now. A recommendation that we set up an interdepartmental committee with fairly broad terms of reference so that at the end of the day we would be in a position to think through all the implications and take a decision based on long-term considerations rather than rush prematurely into precipitate and possibly ill-conceived action that might well have unforeseen repercussions.

[*In other words: No! – Ed.*]

I wasn't prepared to be fobbed off with this nonsense any longer. I told him I wanted *action now*. He went pale. I pointed out that, in my case, honours are fundamentally unhealthy. Nobody in their right mind can want them, they encourage sycophancy, snobbery and jealousy. 'And,' I added firmly, 'it is not fair that civil servants get them all.'

Humphrey argued again. 'We *have* done something to deserve them. We are *civil servants*,' he said.

'You just like having letters to put after your name to impress people,' I sneered. 'You wouldn't impress people if they knew what they stood for: KCB? Knight Commander of the Most Noble Order of the Bath? Bloody daft. They'd think you were a plumber. I think they should shove the whole lot down the Most Noble Order of the Plughole.'

Humphrey wasn't at all amused. 'Very droll,' he said condescendingly. 'You like having letters after your name too,' he continued. 'PC, MP. And your degree – BSc.Econ., I think,' he sneered and slightly wrinkled up his elegant nose as if there were a nasty smell underneath it.

'At least I earned my degree,' I told him, 'not like your MA. At Oxford they give it to you for nothing, when you've got a BA.'

'Not for nothing. For four guineas,' he snapped spitefully.

I was tired of this juvenile bickering. And I had him on the run. I told him that I had made my policy decision and that was the end of it. 'And what was your other point?' I enquired.

Humphrey was in such a state of shock about the Honours List that he had forgotten his other point. But after a few moments it came back to him.

It seems that Baillie College, Oxford, will be in serious trouble over the new ruling on grants for overseas students.

Humphrey said that nothing would please Baillie more than to take British students. *Obviously* that's true. But he explained that Baillie has easily the highest proportion of foreign students and that the repercussions will be serious at the schools of Tropical Medicine and International Law. And the Arabic Department may have to close down completely.

I'm sympathetic to all this, but hard cases make bad law. I just don't see how it's possible for us to go on educating foreigners at the expense of the British taxpayer.

'It's not just foreigners, Minister,' explained Humphrey. 'If, for instance, our Diplomatic Service has nowhere to immerse its recruits in Arab culture, the results could be catastrophic – we might even end up with a pro-Israeli Foreign Office. And what would happen to our oil policy then?'

I said that they could send their diplomatic recruits elsewhere.

'Where else,' he demanded 'can they learn Arabic?'

'Arabia?' I suggested.

He was stumped. Then Bernard chipped in. 'Actually, Minister, Baillie College has an outstanding record. It has filled the jails of the British Empire for many years.'

This didn't sound like much of a recommendation to me. I invited Bernard to explain further.

'As you know,' he said, 'the letters JB are the highest honour in the Commonwealth.'

I didn't know.

Humphrey eagerly explained. 'Jailed by the British. Gandhi, Nkrumah, Makarios, Ben-Gurion, Kenyatta, Nehru, Mugabe – the list of world leaders is endless and contains several of our students.'

Our students? He had said *our* students. It all became clear.

'Which college did you go to, Humphrey?' I smiled benignly.

'Er . . . that is quite beside the point, Minister.'

He wasn't having a very good day. 'I like being beside the point, Humphrey,' I said. 'Humour me. Which college did you go to? Was it Baillie, by any strange coincidence?'

'It so happens,' he admitted with defiance, 'that I am a Baillie man, but that has nothing to do with this.'

I don't know how he has the face to make such a remark. Does he really think I'm a complete idiot? At that moment the buzzer went and saved Humphrey from further humiliation. It was the Division Bell. So I had to hurry off to the House.

On my way out I realised that I had to ask Bernard whether I was to vote 'aye' or 'no'?

'No,' he replied and began to explain. 'It's an Opposition Amendment, the second reading of . . .'

But I had left by then. The boy's a fool. It doesn't matter what the debate *is*, I just don't want to go through the wrong door.

[*Meanwhile, rumours about Hacker's plan to link economies with honours had travelled fast along the two major Whitehall grapevines – the private secretaries' and the drivers'. It was only a matter of hours before news reached Sir Arnold Robinson, the Secretary to the Cabinet. Sir Humphrey was asked to drop in for a chat with Sir Arnold, and an illuminating interview followed – illuminating not only for Sir Humphrey, but also for historians who learn that although the Cabinet Secretary is theoretically* primus inter pares[1] *he is in reality very much* primus. *It seems that all Permanent Secretaries are equal, but some are more equal than others.*

The notes that Sir Arnold made on Sir Humphrey's report have been found among the Civil Service files at Walthamstow and were of course released some years ago under the thirty-year rule.

Sir Humphrey never saw these notes, because no civil servant is shown his own report, except in wholly unusual circumstances – Ed.]

Staff Report (Cont.)   **CR36**

7. LONG TERM POTENTIAL

At present, he/~~she~~ seems

	unlikely to progress further	☑ 1
or	to have potential to rise about one grade but probably no further	☐ 2
or	to have potential to rise two or three grades	☐ 3
or	to have exceptional potential	☐ 4

8. GENERAL REMARKS

Please provide any additional relevant information here, drawing attention to any particular strengths or weaknesses

Told Appleby that I was a little bit worried about this idea of his Minister's, linking Honours to economics.

Appleby said that he could find no effective arguments against this plan.

I indicated that we would regard it as the thin end of the wedge, a Brussels solution. I asked where it would end?

---

[1] First among equals.

Told Appleby that I was a little bit worried about this idea of his Minister's, linking Honours to economies.

Appleby said that he could find no effective arguments against this plan.

I indicated that we would regard it as the thin end of the wedge, a Bennite solution. I asked where it would end?

Appleby replied that he shared my views and had emphasised them to the Minister. He added, somewhat strangely, that the scheme was 'intolerable but yet irresistible'.

I took a dim view. I informed Appleby that, while I was not in any sense reprimanding him, I wanted his assurance that this plan would not be put into practice.

He looked very shaken at the mention of no reprimand. [*Civil Service Code: the mere mention of a reprimand so high up the ladder is severe and deeply wounding criticism. It suggests that the Cabinet Secretary was flying in the face of the 'Good Chap Theory' – the theory that states that 'A Good Chap Does Not Tell A Good Chap What A Good Chap Ought To Know.' Sir Arnold was implying that Sir Humphrey was not a sufficiently good chap. – Ed.*]

Appleby was unable to give me the assurance I required. He merely voiced a hope that Hacker would not be acting on this plan.

I was obliged to point out that hopes are not good enough. If honours were linked to economies in the DAA, the contagion could spread throughout government. To every department.

Again I invited him to say that we could count on him to scotch the scheme. He said he would try. Feeble! I was left with no alternative but to warn him most seriously that, although I was quite sure he knew what he was doing, this matter could cause others to reflect upon whether or not he was sound.

The poor chap seemed to take that very hard – as well he might!

Before I terminated the interview I mentioned that the Master of Baillie, our old college, had been on the phone, and that I was sure Appleby would make sure Hacket treated Baillie as a Special Case.

Appleby seemed no more confident on this matter either, although he said he had arranged for Hacker to be invited to a Benefactor's Dinner.

I congratulated him on his soundness in this matter, which didn't seem to cheer him up a great deal. I begin to think that Appleby is losing his grip – on Hacker at least.

Perhaps Appleby is not an absolutely first-rank candidate to succeed one as Cabinet Secretary. Not really able, in every department. Might do better in a less arduous job, such as chairman of a clearing bank or as an EEC official.

A.R.

[*It is interesting to compare Sir Arnold's report with Sir Humphrey's own account of this interview – Ed.*]

Went over to see Arnold at the Cabinet Office. We got on very well, as usual. He was very concerned about Hacker's idea of linking honours to economies, and almost as concerned about the future of Baillie College. I was on a sticky wicket, but on the whole I think I was able to reassure him that I'm handling these difficult problems as well as anybody could reasonably expect. [*Appleby Papers 31/RJC/638*]

March 26th
[*Hacker's diary resumes – Ed.*]
Today was the Benefactor's Dinner at Baillie College, Oxford, which was, I think, an unqualified success.

For a start, on the way up to Oxford I learned a whole pile of useful gossip from young Bernard.

Apparently Sir Humphrey was summoned by the Cabinet Secretary yesterday and, according to Bernard, got the most frightful wigging.

The Cabinet Secretary really tore him off a strip, because of Bernard's brilliant scheme linking economies to honours.

Interestingly, Bernard continues to refer to it as *my* scheme – on this occasion, because we were in the official car and of course Roy [*The driver – Ed.*] was quietly memorising every word we said, for future buying and selling. No doubt he can sell news of Sir Humphrey's wigging for quite a price in the drivers' pool, though, it should be worth several small leaks in exchange, I should think. So Roy should have some useful snippets in two or three days, which I must remember to extract from him.

I asked Bernard how the Cabinet Secretary actually goes about giving a wigging to someone as high up as Humphrey.

'Normally,' Bernard informed me, 'it's pretty civilised. But this time, apparently, it was no holds barred. Sir Arnold told Sir Humphrey that he wasn't actually reprimanding him!'

'*That* bad?'

'He actually suggested,' Bernard continued, 'that some people might not think Sir Humphrey was sound.'

Roy's ears were out on stalks.

'I see,' I said, with some satisfaction. 'A real punch-up.'

Sir Arnold was so bothered by this whole thing that I wondered if he had a personal stake in it. But I couldn't see why. I presumed he must have his full quota of honours.

I asked Bernard if Arnold already had his G. Bernard nodded. [*You get your G after your K. G is short for Grand Cross. K is a Knighthood. Each department has its own honours. The DAA gets the Bath – Sir Humphrey was, at this time a KCB, and would have been hop-*

ing for his G – thus becoming a Knight Grand Cross of the Bath.

In the FCO the Honours are the Cross of St Michael and St George – CMG, KCMG, and GCMG. The Foreign Office is not popular throughout the rest of the Civil Service, and it is widely held that the CMG stands for 'Call Me God', the KCMG for 'Kindly Call Me God' and the GCMG for 'God Calls Me God' – Ed.]

However, Bernard revealed that although Sir Arnold has indeed got his G, there are numerous honours to which he could still aspire: a peerage, for instance, an OM or a CH, the Order of the Garter, the Knight of the Thistle, etc.

I asked him about the Knight of the Thistle. 'Who do they award the Thistle to, Scotsmen and donkeys?' I enquired wittily.

'There is a distinction,' said Bernard, ever the diplomat.

'You can't have met the Scottish nationalists,' I replied, quick as a flash. I wasn't bothered by Roy's flapping lugs. 'How do they award the Thistle?' I asked.

'A committee sits on it,' said Bernard.

I asked Bernard to brief me about this High Table dinner. 'Does Humphrey *really* think that I will change government policy on University Finance as a result?'

Bernard smiled and said he'd heard Baillie College gives a very good dinner.

We got to Oxford in little over an hour. The M40 is a very good road. So is the M4, come to think of it. I found myself wondering why we've got two really good roads to Oxford before we got any to Southampton, or Dover or Felixstowe or any of the ports.

Bernard explained that nearly all of our Permanent Secretaries were at Oxford. And most Oxford Colleges give you a good dinner.

This seemed incredible – and yet it has the ring of truth about it. 'But did the Cabinet let them get away with this?' I asked.

'Oh no,' Bernard explained. 'They put their foot down. They said there'd be no motorway to take civil servants to dinners in Oxford unless there was a motorway to take Cabinet Ministers hunting in the Shires. That's why when the M1 was built in the fifties it stopped in the middle of Leicestershire.'

There seemed one flaw in this argument. I pointed out that the M11 has only just been completed. 'Don't Cambridge colleges give you a good dinner?'

'Of course,' said Bernard, 'but it's years and years since the Department of Transport had a Permanent Secretary from Cambridge.'

[*It is most interesting to compare Hacker's account of the dinner with Sir Bernard Woolley's recollections of the same event. First, Hacker's version - Ed.*]

The dinner itself went off perfectly.

I knew they wanted to discuss their financial problems, so when we reached the port and walnuts I decided to open up Pandora's Box, let the cat out of the bag and get the ball rolling. [*Hacker never really learned to conquer his mixed metaphor problem – Ed.*] So I remarked that, for a college on the edge of bankruptcy we had not had a bad little dinner. In truth, of course, we'd had a wildly extravagant banquet with four courses and three excellent wines.

The Master countered by informing me that the Fitzwalter Dinner is paid for by a specific endowment – Fitzwalter was a great sixteenth-century benefactor.

The Bursar added that most nights I'd find them eating Mother's Pride[1] and processed cheese.

I remarked that what they need is a twentieth-century benefactor and this innocent remark produced a long lecture on the different types of University benefactors. Isaac Wolfson, apparently, is only the third man in history to have a college named after him at Oxford and Cambridge. Jesus and St John being the first two.

'Benefactors achieve some sort of immortality,' said the Bursar. 'Their names are kept alive and honoured for centuries. Sir William de Vere, whose name was inscribed on a sconce, directed a Baronial army away from Baillie in the fifteenth century – he had the soldiers quartered at St George's College instead.'

I didn't want to appear ignorant, but I ventured a comment that I didn't actually know there was a St George's College. 'There isn't,' said the Bursar, 'not any more.'

We all chuckled.

Then the Bursar told me about Henry Monkton.

'The Monkton Quad is named after him. He stopped Cromwell from melting down the college silver to pay for the New Model Army.'

Humphrey added:

'Told them that the silver was much better quality at Trinity, Cambridge.'

More chuckles all round. Then the Master pointedly remarked that it now looked as if there'd be no college left to remember these

---

[1] Brand name of popular packaged sliced loaf, not of the kind customarily consumed at High Table.

benefactors. Unless the problem of the overseas students can be solved.

They all looked at me and waited. I'm used to this kind of pressure, but naturally I wanted to help if I could. So I explained that one *always* tries to help and that politicians only go into politics out of a desire to help others. I explained that I'm an idealist. And, in case they were under the impression that all this talk of honouring benefactors might persuade me to help Baillie in some way, I pointed out that any honour is irrelevant to me – after all, there's not much point in having your name on a silver sconce when you're six feet under.

Humphrey changed the conversation abruptly at that moment, and started asking when the University awards its honorary doctorates.

The Master said that the ceremony isn't for a few months but the Senate makes its final selection in a matter of weeks.

I don't think that it was entirely coincidental that Humphrey mentioned this matter at this juncture.

[*The ceremony in question takes place each June. A large luncheon is given in the Codrington Library of All Souls, followed by an afternoon reception. The degrees are given in a Latin ceremony, in the Sheldonian. All the speeches are in Latin. The Chancellor of the University was, at this period that arch-manipulator of politicians and, with Sir Harold Wilson, Joint Life President of the Society of Electoral Engineers: Mr Harold Macmillan – Ed.*].

Humphrey, the Master, and the Bursar were – I realised – hinting at an offer. Not an unattractive one. I've always secretly regretted not being an Oxbridge man, as I am undoubtedly of sufficient intellectual calibre. And there must be very few LSE men who've ever had an honorary degree from Oxford.

The Master dropped another hint. Very decorously. He said that there was still one honorary doctorate of Law to decide, and that he and his colleagues were wondering whether it should go to a judge or to someone in government!

I suggested that someone in government might be more appropriate. Perhaps as a tribute to the Chancellor of the University. I know that I argued it rather brilliantly, because they were so enthusiastic and warm in response to me – but I can't actually remember precisely how I put it.

Exhausted by the intellectual cut and thrust of the evening, I fell asleep in the car going home.

SIR BERNARD WOOLLEY RECALLS[1]:

Having seen Hacker's account of this dinner, and his behaviour at it, I'm afraid to say that it is rather inaccurate and self-serving.

By the time we had reached the port Hacker was, not to put too fine a point on it, embarrassingly drunk.

The Master, Sir Humphrey and several of the dons set about persuading him that he would acquire a certain immortality if he became a college benefactor – in other words, if he made Baillie a special case in the matter of overseas students. A typical Oxford 'you scratch my back, I'll scratch yours' offer.

Hacker's reference to the conversation about Wolfson and Jesus Colleges is less than complete. When told that Wolfson is the only man, other than Jesus and St John, to have colleges named after them at both Oxford and Cambridge, he looked glassy-eyed and blank. 'Jesus?' he asked. The Bursar actually felt called upon to clarify it. 'Jesus *Christ*, that is,' he added.

When Hacker remarked that he wanted to help he was pouring himself a glass of port. His actual words, I clearly recall, were 'Yes, well, one would certainly like to help oneself . . . I mean, help one's friends, that is, help the college . . . not for the honours of course . . .'. Completely transparent.

The Master and Bursar chimed in with suitable bromides like 'Perish the thought,' 'Ignoble suggestion.'

Hacker then gave us all that guff about how he was in politics to help others, and how he wasn't interested in honours – but when the honorary doctorates were mentioned he got so excited he cracked a walnut so hard that pieces of shell were flying across High Table like shrapnel.

Then came his final humiliation.

By the time the matter was raised as to whether the last remaining honorary doctorate (if indeed it were so) should go to a judge or a politician, it was clear that the academics were playing games with Hacker.

He was too drunk to see that they were merely amusing themselves. I well remember the appalling drunken speech he launched into. It is forever etched on my memory.

He began by saying 'Judge? You don't want to make a judge a doctor of law. Politicians,' he said, 'are the ones who make the laws. And pass the laws,' he added, apparently unaware of the tautology. 'If it wasn't for politicians, judges wouldn't be able to do any judging, they wouldn't have any laws to judge, know what I mean? They'd all be out of work. Queues of unemployed judges. In silly wigs.'

I remember that argument well because the idea of unemployed judges in silly wigs richly appealed to me, as it would to anyone who has had contact with the higher and more self-satisfied reaches of the legal profession. In fact, I have always been struck by the absurdity of judges ticking people off in court about their unsuitable appearance – women in trousers, for instance – while the judges, themselves are in fancy dress.

Be that as it may, Hacker continued in the cringing self-pitying

[1] In conversation with the Editors.

lacrymose manner that he only exhibited when completely sloshed.

'Anyway, it's easy for the judges,' he whined, 'they don't have to suck up to television producers. Don't have to lie to journalists. Don't have to pretend to like their Cabinet colleagues. Do you know something?' he cracked another walnut and a piece of deadly flying shell struck the Bursar just below the left eye. 'If judges had to put up with some of my Cabinet colleagues we'd have the death penalty back tomorrow. Good job too.'

By this time old Sir Humphrey was trying to stem the flow – but to no avail.

For Hacker pointed accusingly at Sir Humphrey. 'And I'll tell you another thing,' he said, sublimely unaware that nobody at the table wanted to hear another thing, 'I can't send you to prison.'

Humphrey was flummoxed by this remark.

Hacker looked around the table. 'I can't send him to prison,' he said, as if he had revealed a new extraordinary anomaly in the law. 'But if I were a judge, I could whizz old Humphrey off to the Scrubs, no trouble, feet wouldn't touch the ground, clang bang, see you in three years time, one-third remission for good conduct.'

Everyone was now staring at Hacker, open-mouthed, as he paused for breath, slurped at his glass and some Fonseca 1927 dribbled slowly down his chin. Being academics, they had hardly ever seen a politician in action late at night. [*Hacker's behaviour, of course, would have passed unnoticed at the House of Commons, where it would have been accepted as quite normal – possibly, even better than average. – Ed.*]

Hacker was still talking. Now he was unstoppable. 'But I can't do that to old Humphrey,' he raved incoherently. 'I have to listen to him – Oh God!' He looked at the ceiling, and seemed to be on the verge of tears. 'He goes *on* and *on*. Do you know, his sentences are longer than Judge Jeffries?' He guffawed. We stared at him. 'No, no, to sum up, politicians are much more deserving, you don't want to give your donorary hoctorates to judges . . . definitely not.'

Finally he ground to a halt. The Master hastily pulled himself together and tried to rearrange his features from disgust to friendliness. He was only partially successful.

Nevertheless he managed to tell Hacker that he had argued the proposition beautifully, and that he now realised that the honour couldn't possibly go to a judge.

There were mutters of agreement all round, as the dons continued their embarrassing flattery of Hacker. No one really understands the true nature of fawning servility until he has seen an academic who has glimpsed the prospect of money. Or personal publicity.

They went on to say how wonderful it would be to see Hacker standing there, in the Sheldonian, wearing magnificent crimson robes, receiving the doctorate in front of a packed assembly of eminent scholars such as himself. Hacker belched, alcoholic fumes emanated from his mouth, his eyes went glassy, clutched his chair so that he wouldn't fall on to the floor, and he smiled beatifically.

I have always remembered that night. I took one more step towards maturity as I realised that even the most rigorous academics have their price – and it's not as high as you'd think.

[*Hacker's diary continues – Ed.*]

March 27th

Had rather a headache this morning. I don't know why, it can't be a hangover as I didn't drink all that much last night. I couldn't have done or I wouldn't have been such a success.

We were due to have yet another meeting to examine the possibility of administrative cuts. But the outcome was sure to be the same as last time.

Humphrey popped into my office five minutes early, for a private word. Very good news. Apparently the Master of Baillie took Humphrey aside last night and asked him to sound me out, to see if I'd be interested in accepting an honorary doctorate of Law from the University.

I feigned surprise. In fact I wasn't at all surprised, as I knew what an impression I'd made on them last night.

Humphrey was at pains to point out that it was not an actual offer. Apparently, according to Humphrey, the Council of the Senate or somebody or other is now trying to square the honorary doctorate with my well-known hostility to honours.

This was a bit of a blow. I had to squash this nonsense at once. 'Don't be silly, Humphrey, that's quite different,' I explained.

'Not entirely Minister,' he replied. 'It is a matter of accepting a doctorate without having done anything to earn it, as you yourself might put it in your refreshingly blunt fashion.'

'I'm a Cabinet Minister,' I responded with some indignation.

'Isn't that what you're paid for?' Smooth treacherous bugger.

'The point is,' I told him, 'one can't really refuse an honorary doctorate. I should have thought anyone could see that I would be insulting the DAA if I refused – because clearly I've been offered it as a sort of vote of confidence in the Department because I am, in fact, the titular head.'

Humphrey fell silent, having indicated again that it was not yet an offer. Clearly he had some sort of deal in mind. I waited. And waited.

Then the penny dropped. 'By the way, Humphrey,' I said breezily. 'Changing the subject *entirely*, I would like to do what I can to help Baillie College over this overseas student problem.'

Now it was Humphrey's turn to feign surprise. 'Oh, good,' he said, and smiled.

I explained quietly, however, that we need a reason. By which I meant a pretext. He was ready with one, as I knew he would be.

'No problem. I understand that the Palace has been under pressure from a number of Commonwealth leaders. We can't embarrass the Palace, so we'll have to redesignate Baillie as a Commonwealth Education Centre.'

Immediately I saw a chance for the deal that *I* wanted to do.

'But how will I find the money?' I asked wide-eyed. 'You know how set I am on making five per cent cuts across the board. If we could achieve that . . . well, anything's possible.'

I reckoned that this was an offer he couldn't refuse. I was right. 'We *might* be able to achieve these cuts —' this was a big step forward — 'and I can only speak for this department, of course, as long as this absurd idea of linking cuts to honours were to be shelved.'

So there it was. A double *quid pro quo*. Out in the open.

The expenditure Survey Committee gathered around my conference table.

The minutes of the last meeting went through on the nod. Then we came to Matters Arising. The first was *Accommodation*. Sir Humphrey pre-empted the Assistant Secretary who usually spoke on this matter. As the young man opened his mouth to reply, I heard Humphrey's voice: 'I'm happy to say that we have found a five per cent cut by selling an old office block in High Wycombe.'

The Assistant Secretary looked mightily surprised. Clearly Humphrey had not forewarned him of the New Deal.

I was delighted. I said so. We moved straight on to number two: *Stationery Acquisition*.

A Deputy Secretary spoke up, after getting an unmistakeable eye signal and slight nod of the head from Humphrey. 'Yes, we'd discovered that a new stock control system will reduce expenditure this year.'

'By how much?' I asked.

The Deputy Secretary hesitated uncertainly. 'About five per cent, wasn't it?' said Humphrey smoothly.

The Dep. Sec. muttered his agreement.

'Good, good,' I said. 'Three: *Parks and Forestry Administration?*'

An Under-Secretary spoke, having caught on with the civil servant's customary speed to a change in the party line.

'If we delay the planned new computer installation, we can make a saving there.'

'Can we?' I said, pretending surprise. 'How much?'

They all pretended that they couldn't remember. Much consultation of paper and files.

A bright Principal spoke up: 'About five per cent?' he said, hopefully. We all nodded our approval, and assorted civil servants muttered 'Of that order.'

Humphrey pointed out that the saving in the computer installation would lead inevitably to a cut in *Data Processing* I looked at him expectantly. 'By about five per cent,' he said.

'This is all very encouraging, Humphrey,' I said benevolently.

And after the meeting, at which everyone had somehow managed to come up with cuts of about five per cent, Humphrey took me aside for a quiet word.

'Minister, while I think of it, have you finished with the list of departmental recommendations to the Honours Secretary?'

'Certainly.' I was at my most obliging. 'There was no problem with any of them. Bernard will give it to you. All right, Humphrey?'

'Yes, Doctor,' he replied.

A fitting tribute. I look forward to the ceremony next June.

3
The Death List

March 28th

It's become clear to me, as I sit here for my usual Sunday evening period of contemplation and reflection, that Roy (my driver) knows a great deal more than I realised about what is going on in Whitehall.

Whitehall is the most secretive square mile in the world. The great emphasis on avoidance of error (which is what the Civil Service is really about, since that is their only real incentive) also means that avoidance of publication is equally necessary.

As Sir Arnold is reported to have said some months ago, 'If no one knows what you're doing, then no one knows what you're doing *wrong.*'

[*Perhaps this explains why government forms are always so hard to understand. Forms are written to protect the person who is in charge of the form – Ed.*]

And so the way information is provided – or withheld – is the key to running the government smoothly.

This concern with the avoidance of error leads inexorably to the need to commit everything to paper – civil servants copy *everything*, and send copies to all their colleagues. (This is also because 'chaps don't like to leave other chaps out', as Bernard once explained to me.) The Treasury was rather more competent before the invention of Xerox than it is now, because its officials had so much less to read (and therefore less to confuse them).

The civil servants hunger for paper is insatiable. They want all possible information sent to them, and they send all possible information to their colleagues. It amazes me that they find the time to do anything other than catch up with other people's paperwork. If indeed they do.

It is also astonishing that so little of this vast mass of typescript ever becomes public knowledge – a very real tribute to Whitehall's talent for secrecy. For it is axiomatic with civil servants that information should only be revealed to their political 'masters' when absolutely necessary, and to the public when absolutely unavoidable.

But I now see that I can learn some useful lessons from their methods. For a start, I must pay more attention to Bernard and Roy. I resolve today that I will not let false pride come between Roy and me – in other words, I shall no longer pretend that I know more than my driver does. Tomorrow, when he collects me at Euston, I shall ask him to tell me anything that he has picked up, and I shall tell him that he mustn't assume that Ministers know more secrets than drivers.

On second thoughts, I don't need to tell him that – he knows already!

As to the Private Secretaries' grapevine, it was most interesting to learn last week that Sir Humphrey had had a wigging from Sir Arnold. This will have profoundly upset Humphrey, who above all values the opinions of his colleagues.

For there is one grapevine with even more knowledge and influence than the Private Secretaries' or the drivers' – and that is the Permanent Secretaries' Grapevine. (Cabinet colleagues, of course, have a hopeless grapevine because they are not personal friends, don't know each other all that well, and hardly ever see each other except in Cabinet or in the Division Lobby.)

This wigging could also, I gather, affect his chances of becoming Secretary to the Cabinet on Arnold's retirement, or screw up the possibility of his finding a cushy job in Brussels.

Happily, this is not my problem – and, when I mentioned it to my spies, both Bernard and Roy agreed (independently) that Sir Humphrey would not be left destitute. Apart from his massive index-linked pension, a former Permanent Secretary is always fixed up with a job if he wants it – Canals and Waterways, or *something*.

As for Bernard, I have recently been impressed with his loyalty to me. He seems to be giving me all the help he possibly can without putting his own career at risk. In fact, I am almost becoming concerned about the amount of rapport, decency and goodwill that exists between us – if he exhibits a great deal more of these qualities he will almost certainly be moved elsewhere. There may come a time when the Department feels that the more use he is to *me* the less use he is to *them*.

March 29th

I was sitting at my desk this afternoon going through some letters when Bernard sidled in holding something behind his back.

'Excuse me Minister,' he said. 'There's something in the press about you that I think you ought to see.'

I was pleased. 'About me? That's nice.'

Bernard looked bleak. 'Well . . .' he swallowed, 'I'm afraid it's in *Private Eye*.'

Trembling, I took the offending rag and held it away from me with my forefinger and thumb. I didn't have the courage to open it. Normally the Press Officer brings you your own press cuttings. If he'd given his job to Bernard, it meant terrible news. No prizes for guessing which, in the case of *Private Eye*.

'They're . . . um . . . exposing something,' said Bernard.

Panic thoughts flashed through my mind. In that instant my whole life passed before me. Was it that IOS Consultancy, I wondered? Or that character reference I wrote for Dr Savundra? Or that wretched party at John Poulson's?

I didn't even dare mention them to Bernard. So I put a good face on it. 'Well,' I said, chin up, 'what have they made up about me to put in their squalid little rag?'

'Perhaps you'd better read it yourself,' he said.

So I did.

It was acutely embarrassing.

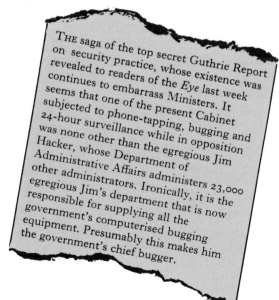

THE saga of the top secret Guthrie Report on security practice, whose existence was revealed to readers of the *Eye* last week continues to embarrass Ministers. It seems that one of the present Cabinet subjected to phone-tapping, bugging and 24-hour surveillance while in opposition was none other than the egregious Jim Hacker, whose Department of Administrative Affairs administers 23,000 other administrators. Ironically, it is the egregious Jim's department that is now responsible for supplying all the government's computerised bugging equipment. Presumably this makes him the government's chief bugger.

I sent for Humphrey at once. I had to establish whether or not this lie was true.

One aspect of this squalid little story puzzled me in particular – 'What does egregious mean?' I asked Bernard.

'I think it means "outstanding" . . . in one way or another,' he explained.

That's okay, *if* that's what it means, but it seems a little too generous for *Private Eye*. I must remember to look it up sometime.

Humphrey arrived, was shown the piece, and actually had the temerity to laugh at the bugger joke.

'Is this true?' I demanded.

'Oh absolutely not, Minister,' he replied firmly. I was relieved for a moment, until he went on, 'it's only one of their little jokes. I don't think that anyone actually supposes that you are a bu . . . I mean . . . that is . . .'

I exploded. 'Humphrey, I'm not talking about that tasteless little joke. I'm asking you if the gist of this story is true – was I once under surveillance and am I now responsible for the bugging equipment?'

'Surely . . .' said Humphrey evasively, and how well I recognise the tactics by now! 'Surely you don't believe what you read in that squalid little rag?'

[*'Squalid little rag' was clearly Whitehall general slang usage for* Private Eye *at about this time – Ed.*]

I asked him again. Was it accurate?

Sir Humphrey again declined to give a straight answer. 'I don't think we should take it too seriously, Minister,' he replied suavely.

I saw red. I told him that I regard this as an outrageous and intolerable intrusion into my privacy. If he didn't see anything wrong with it, I certainly did. And I propose to take it very seriously indeed. I reminded Humphrey that the article stated that I, a free citizen, and furthermore an MP, have been under total surveillance. Surveillance is an attack on democracy. I asked Humphrey if he was aware that it contravenes the European Convention on Human Rights.

He remained calm. 'Surveillance,' he said, 'is an indispensable weapon in the battle against organised crime.'

I was incredulous. That's no reason for bugging me, a politician. 'Humphrey,' I asked, 'are you describing politicians as organised crime?'

He smiled. 'Well . . . disorganised crime too,' he joked. I was not amused. He realised that he was going too far, and hastily started to repair the damage. 'No, seriously, Minister . . .'

I cut him short. I reminded Humphrey of my own track-record, one which made this situation particularly awkward for me.

'While I was editor of *Reform* I wrote a leader criticising this kind of intrusion. Furthermore, I started a nationwide petition against bureaucratic busybodies snooping and phone-tapping. And *now* I learn,' I continued angrily '— from *Private Eye*, please note, and not from you – that *I*, of *all* people, am in charge of the whole technical side of it.' It was all profoundly embarrassing.

Sir Humphrey merely nodded.

I asked the inevitable question.

'Why didn't you tell me about this?'

'Because,' came the inevitable answer, 'you didn't ask.'

'Well,' I said, 'thank God for the free press. Thank God for at least one brave, open and fearless journal in this country.'

Bernard started to remind me that I had previously described it differently, but I stopped him. However, I took the opportunity to explain to him that he really must sharpen up his political antennae. He needs to learn to adjust more flexibly to a developing situation.

He took my point, I think – I hope!

The next question inevitably raised by these revelations concerns the tapes and/or transcripts that must have been made of my bugged conversations. Where are they?

'I imagine,' said Humphrey carelessly, as if it didn't really matter all that much, 'that they must have been put into a report.'

'And who got those reports?' I wanted to know.

'I imagine that the Home Secretary gets . . . got them.' He corrected himself quickly. But not quickly enough.

'*Gets* them?' I shrieked. 'You mean it's *still going on?*'

He tried to pacify me, but without success. 'No, Minister, not you, not now. *Now* he will be getting reports on current members of Her Majesty's Opposition.'

The mechanics were still unclear to me. 'Who gives these reports to the Home Secretary?' I demanded.

He shrugged. 'MI5, presumably.'

'You seem very calm about all this.'

He smiled. He was really getting right up my nose, the complacent . . . [*expletive deleted – Ed.*]

I certainly wasn't calm about it. I threw one of my real fits. I denounced the whole business. 'It is *horrifying*,' I insisted. 'A British citizen – in my case, a *distinguished* British citizen – one who has dedicated his life to the service of his fellow countrymen . . . and all the time those gloating, faceless bureaucrats are listening to his every word. All his private calls. His rows with his wife. His shouting matches with his daughter. His private arrangements with his accountant.' Perhaps I'd gone too far – maybe the room was bugged! 'Not that I have anything I'd be ashamed to reveal, my life is an open book.'

'Quite, quite,' agreed both Humphrey and Bernard.

'But it's the principle of the thing!'

I stopped. I waited. The ball was in his court. Surely Sir Humphrey would have something to say. But no explanation or justification was forthcoming.

Sir Humphrey just sat there, head sympathetically inclined to one side, listening, for all the world like a Freudian psychoanalyst who has been sitting at the head of a couch listening to the rantings and ravings of a neurotic patient.

After he'd said nothing for quite a long time, I realised that he *didn't* realise that the ball was in his court.

'Why?' I asked.

Sir Humphrey jumped, and focussed his eyes in my direction. 'Why what?' he replied. 'Why surveillance, or why you?'

'Both.'

'In any case,' he smiled blandly, 'it's the same answer.'

My blood boiled. 'Then why,' I snapped, 'did you split it into two questions?'

There was no reply to that.

[*Sir Humphrey could hardly explain to Hacker that he did not want to risk answering a question that Hacker had not asked – Ed.*]

Then Humphrey began his general explanation. 'I should have thought it was perfectly obvious. Before the election it was rumoured that you might be appointed Secretary of State for Defence. If the PM were to consider giving you Defence, you can surely see that it would be in the national interest for MI5 to satisfy itself that you were not a security risk?'

'But my privacy was invaded,' I pointed out.

He smiled his smuggest smile. 'Better than your country being invaded, Minister.'

I must say, I could see that point. There was a valid argument there.

But I was sure that Humphrey had never experienced the feeling that I was feeling. And democracy is about the feelings and rights of the individual – that's what distinguishes a democracy from a dictatorship.

I said to him: 'Have *you* ever been under surveillance, Humphrey?'

He was astounded. 'Me?'

'You. You, Humphrey.'

He got on to his highest horse. 'I am a civil servant,' he said, as if that absolutely closed the discussion.

'So were Burgess and Maclean, and Philby,' I observed.

He was rattled, but he swiftly produced a counter-argument. 'They were not Permanent Secretaries! One becomes a Permanent Secretary only after a lifetime of personal responsibility, reliability and integrity. The most rigorous selection procedures winnow out all but the most upright, honourable and discreet of public servants.'

I noted the emphasis on 'discreet'. The secrecy thing again, here openly acknowledged. I also noted that in giving this glowing description of Permanent Secretaries he thought that he was, in fact, describing himself. And I also noted that he had begged the question: even if Permanent Secretaries are never security risks, Humphrey said that he had *never* been bugged. But he hasn't been a Permanent Secretary all his life, has he?

As Humphrey had described the qualities of Permanent Secretaries in a way that argued that they need not be subject to surveillance, I inquired how he felt about Ministers. It was as I expected.

'Ministers,' he said, 'have a whole range of dazzling qualities including . . . um . . . well, including an enviable intellectual suppleness and moral manoeuvrability.'

I invited him to explain himself.

'You can't trust Ministers,' he said bluntly. I was appalled at his rudeness. 'I'm being quite candid now,' he added unnecessarily. Bloody insolent, I'd call it. 'I don't mean, by the way, that we can't trust *you*, Minister – of course we can. But in general terms Ministers, unlike civil servants, are selected completely at random – by Prime Ministerial whim, in recognition of doubtful favours received, or to avoid appointing someone of real ability who might become a threat – not *you*, of course, Minister. *You* can certainly be trusted. *You* might almost be a civil servant yourself.'

[*Sir Humphrey almost certainly meant this as a compliment. Indeed, the ultimate compliment. However, Hacker should certainly have taken this as a hint that he might be house trained. Regrettably, he allowed the flattery to get the better of him – Ed.*]

I was mollified. I didn't think he was bullshitting.

I let him continue. 'Minister, would you trust every one of your Cabinet colleagues never to betray a confidence?'

I couldn't really give an answer to that, without appearing somewhat disloyal to my Cabinet colleagues.

'And what about all the Opposition Front Bench?' he asked.

That was an easy one. 'You certainly can't trust that lot,' I exclaimed.

'Quite so,' he said, checkmating me neatly, 'and *you* were on the Opposition Front Bench at the time.'

It has always been hard to win this kind of argument with Humphrey. But he's into winning arguments – whereas I'm into getting things done!

So I cut the discussion short. I made my decision. Which is to stop all surveillance. It's a matter of principle.

He countered by informing me that this is a Home Office matter, and in many cases not within our purview.

This didn't bother me. I can certainly make it much more difficult in future. If I'm responsible for the apparatus, I intend to make myself responsible for some proper democratic safeguards for us all (before the apparatus can be used).

'Are you perhaps going to suggest,' he enquired sarcastically, 'that people will not be able to be put under secret surveillance until they've signed a form saying that they agree to it?'

I rose above it. 'No,' I said gently but firmly, 'I propose that we shall have a Select Committee of both Houses chaired by a Law Lord to decide on every application. And no surveillance will be allowed to go on for more than two weeks without reapplying.'

Then I told him to set the wheels in motion.

He argued no further, but took his leave of me in a very frosty manner.

I was full of ideas today. After Humphrey had stalked out I told Bernard to send a Minute to each member of the Cabinet.

I also thought of planting a question from one of our back-benchers to the Home Secretary. Something like: *Will the Home Secretary assure the House that none of his Cabinet colleagues has ever been placed under government surveillance?* That will shake him. And it will bring the matter out into the open. We'll see if it's just a Home Office matter! I think not!

Finally, I asked Bernard to make an appointment for me to meet Walter Fowler of the *Express* for a quick drink in Annie's Bar at the

House, later this week.

'What for?' Bernard wanted to know.

'First law of political indiscretion,' I replied. 'You always have a drink before you leak.'

[*Walter Fowler was the Lobby Correspondent of the* Express. *This meant that he would probably have been their political editor or head of the paper's political staff. The Lobby was a uniquely British system, the best way yet devised in any democracy for taming and muzzling the press.*

This is because it is hard to censor the press when it wants to be free, but easy if it gives up its freedom voluntarily.

There were in the 1980s 150 Lobby Correspondents, who had the special privilege of being able to mingle with MPs and Ministers in the Lobby behind both chambers of Parliament. As journalists, however, they were – quite properly – not allowed to sit down on the leather-covered benches. Neither were they allowed to report anything they saw – e.g. MPs hitting one another – nor anything they overheard.

You may ask: who stipulated what they were not allowed to do? Who made all these restrictions? Answer: The lobby correspondents themselves!

In return for the freedom of access to Ministers, and MPs they exercised the most surprising and elaborate self-censorship.

The Lobby received daily briefings from the Prime Minister's Press Secretary at Number 10 Downing Street, and weekly briefings from the Leader of the House and the Leader of the Opposition. All these briefings were unattributable.

The Lobby correspondents argued that, in return for their self-censorship, they would learn infinitely more about the government, its motives, and its plans. The politicians loved the Lobby system because they could leak any old rubbish, which the Lobby would generally swallow whole. As they had heard it in confidence, they believed it must be true.

We believe, with the advantage of hindsight, that the Lobby was merely one example of the way in which the British establishment dealt with potential danger or criticism – it would embrace the danger, and thus suffocate it.

The Lobby certainly discouraged political journalists from going out and searching for a story, as they only had to sit on their bottoms in Annie's Bar (the bar exclusively reserved for the press, with the highest alcoholic consumption of any of the thirteen bars within the Palace of Westminster – which was saying something!) and a 'leak' would come their way.

Finally, a word on leaks. Because there was no free access to information in Whitehall, everybody leaked. Everybody knew there was no other way to make the wheels go round.

Equally, everybody pretended that leaking was 'not on', 'not cricket', 'below board' or underhand in the same way. This is because discretion is the most highly valued talent in Whitehall. Even above 'soundness'. Or perhaps discretion is the ultimate indication that you are 'sound'!

Whenever a 'leak' occurred there would be cries of moral indignation, and a leak inquiry would be set up by the Prime Minister. Such enquiries seldom reported at the end, for fear of the embarrassing result – most leaks came from 'Number Ten' (a euphemism), most budget leaks from 'Number Eleven' (another euphemism) – Ed.]

March 30th

I met Walter Fowler in Annie's Bar, as arranged, and leaked my plans for curtailing surveillance.

Walter seemed a little sceptical. He said it was a worthy cause but I'd never see it through. This made me all the more determined. I told him that I intended to see it through, and to carry the Home Office on this matter in due course. I asked him if it would make a story – I knew it would, but journalists like to feel that their opinions are valuable.

Walter confirmed it would make a story: 'MINISTER FIGHTS FOR PHONE-TAP SAFE GUARDS – yes, there's something there.' He wheezed deeply and drank two-thirds of a pint of special.

I asked where they'd run it. He thought fairly high up on the Home News Page. I was slightly disappointed.

'Not on page one?'

'Well . . .' said Walter doubtfully. 'Can I attribute it? MINISTER SPEAKS OUT!'

I squashed that at once.

'So where did I get the story?' asked Walter plaintively. 'I presume I can't say it was "officially announced" or a "government spokesman"?'

I told him he presumed right.

We silently pondered the other options.

'How about "sources close to the Minister"?' he asked after a minute or two.

'Hopeless,' I pointed out, 'I don't want *everybody* to know I told you. Isn't it possible for you to do a "speculation is growing in West-minster . . ."?'

Walter shook his head sadly. 'Bit weak,' he said, and again he wheezed. He was like an old accordion. He produced a vile-looking pipe from his grubby pockets and stuffed tobacco into the bowl with a stubby forefinger that had a thick black line of dirt under the nail.

I watched fascinated. 'What about "unofficial spokesman",' I suggested, just before the first gust of smoke engulfed me.

'I've used that twice this week already,' replied Walter, con-tentedly polluting the atmosphere of central London. I choked quietly.

It was true. He had used it twice this week. I'd noticed. 'Cabinet's leaking like a sieve, isn't it?'

He nodded. 'Yes – um . . .' he poured some more bitter past his nicotine-stained molars into his smoking mouth, '. . . could we attribute it to a leading member of the sieve?' I looked at him. 'Er . . . Cabinet,' he corrected himself hastily.

I shook my head.

'How would you like to be an "informed source"?' he offered.

That seemed a good idea. I hadn't been an informed source for some weeks.

'Okay,' I said. 'That's what I'll be.'

Walter chuckled. 'Quite a joke, isn't it?'

'What?' I asked blankly.

'Describing someone as "informed", when his Permanent Secret-ary is Sir Humphrey Appleby.'

He bared his yellow teeth at me. I think it was a smile. I didn't smile back – I just bared my teeth at him.

March 31st

Annie came up to London today from the constituency.

So this evening I told her about the surveillance we'd been under. I thought she'd be as indignant as me. But she didn't seem to care.

I tried to make her grasp the extent of the wrongdoing. 'Every-thing we said on the phone, everything we said to each other – all re-corded. Transcribed. It's humiliating.'

'Yes, I see . . .' she said thoughtfully, 'it is a little humiliating that someone at MI5 knows just how boring our life is.'

'What?'

'All will be revealed,' she said. 'Or has already been revealed. That what you talk about at home is what you talk about in public –

the gross national product, the public sector borrowing require-
ment, the draft agenda for the party conference . . .'

I explained that I didn't mean *that*. I meant that all our private
family talk had been overheard.

'Oh dear, yes,' said Annie. 'I hadn't thought of that . . . "Have you
got the car keys?" . . . "No, I thought *you* had them" . . . "No, I gave
them to you" . . . My God, that could bring the government down!'

'Annie.' I was cross. 'You're not taking this seriously.'

'Whatever gives you that idea?'

'You still haven't grasped how our privacy had been intruded
upon. They might have heard what we say to each other . . . in bed.'

'Would it matter?' she asked, feigning surprise. 'Do you snore in
code?'

I think she was trying to tell me something. Only last week she
caused me great embarrassment when she was interviewed in some
juvenile woman's magazine. They asked her if the earth moved
when she went to bed with me. 'No,' she'd replied, 'not even the
bed moves.'

Perhaps this was part of a campaign.

It was. She went on. 'Look, it's the Bank Holiday weekend coming up. Why don't we go away for a long weekend, two or three
days, like we used to?'

My first thought was that I couldn't. Then I thought: why not?
And I couldn't think of a reason. After all, even statesmen need
holidays. I agreed.

'Let's go to Kingsbury Down,' she said.

'Fine,' I said. 'Where is it?'

She stared at me. 'Only where we spent our honeymoon, darling.'
Funny, I'd forgotten the name of the place. I tried to remember
what it looked like.

'It's where you first explained to me your theory about the effect
of velocity of circulation on the net growth of the money supply.'

I remembered it well. 'Oh yes, I know the place then,' I said.

Annie turned towards her bedside lamp. 'Did you get that, boys?'
she muttered into it.

[*A startling development took place on the following day. The
Special Branch contacted Sir Humphrey Appleby and Bernard Wool-
ley with the news that a terrorist hit list had been discovered, and Jim
Hacker's name appeared on it as a potential target.*

*The list apparently was drawn up by a group calling itself the Inter-
national Freedom Army – Ed.*]

SIR BERNARD WOOLLEY RECALLS[1]:
We could not imagine who on earth could possibly want to assassinate the Minister. He was so harmless.

Nevertheless, Sir Humphrey Appleby and I were fully agreed that it was not possible to take risks with the Minister's life, and so the whole paraphernalia of security would have to be brought out to protect him.

[*Hacker's diary continues – Ed.*]

April 2nd
Bernard greeted me like a mother hen this morning. He asked after my health with an earnest and solicitous attitude.

I thought perhaps it was because I was a little late at the office. I hadn't slept too well – 'I feel like death,' I remarked.

Bernard whispered to Sir Humphrey, 'Perhaps that's just as well,' a comment which I did not understand at the time but which I now regard as having been in the poorest of taste.

I was actually rather cheerful. My leak had worked. A story had appeared in the *Express*: HACKER MOVES TO CURB PHONE TAPS. I was described as an informed source, as agreed, and Walter had not taken a bye-line – the story was 'from our Political Staff'.

Sir Humphrey wondered audibly where they'd got the information, and stared at me. Naturally I admitted nothing.

[*It has been said that the ship of state is the only type of ship that leaks from the top – Ed.*]

'Anyway,' I added, 'this leak only confirms my determination to act on this matter.'

Humphrey asked me if I'd considered all the implications. This is generally the Civil Service way of asking me if I realised that I was talking rubbish. In this case, as it was to turn out, I had *not* quite considered all the implications.

So I replied that free citizens have a right to privacy. An absolute right.

How could I have said such a thing?

But I didn't know then what I knew just five minutes later. Those bastards hadn't told me.

'Suppose . . .' suggested Sir Humphrey smoothly, 'suppose MI5 had reason to suspect that these "free citizens" were, shall we say to take a purely hypothetical example, planning to assassinate a Minister of the Crown?'

---

[1] In conversation with the Editors.

I made a little speech. I spoke of the freedom of the British people, and how this is more important than the lives of a few Ministers. I said that freedom is indivisible, whereas Ministers are expendable. 'Men in public life must expect to be the targets of cranks and fanatics. A Minister has the duty to set his own life at naught, to stand up and say "Here I am, do your worst!" and not cower in craven terror behind electronic equipment and secret microphones and all the hideous apparatus of the police state.' Me and my big mouth.

Sir Humphrey and Bernard looked at each other. The former tried to speak but I made it clear that I would brook no arguments.

'No Humphrey, I don't want to hear any more about it. You deal in evasions and secrets. But politicians in a free country must be seen to be the champions of freedom and truth. Don't try and give me the arguments in favour of telephone tapping – I can find them in Stalin's memoirs.'

'Actually,' quibbled Bernard, 'Stalin didn't write any memoirs. He was too secretive. He was afraid people might read them.'

Humphrey finally succeeded in interrupting us.

'Minister,' he insisted, 'you *must* allow me to say one more thing on this matter.'

I told him that he might say one sentence, but he should keep it brief.

'The Special Branch have found your name on a death list,' he said.

I thought I must have misheard.

'What?' I said.

'The Special Branch have found your name on a death list,' he repeated.

This made no sense. A death list? Why me?

'A death list?' I asked. 'What do you mean, a death list?'

'An assassination list,' he said.

He really is a fool. 'I know what you mean by a death list,' I said, 'but . . . what do you mean?'

Sir Humphrey was now as baffled as I.

'I don't know how I can express it more clearly, Minister,' he said plaintively.

Obviously, I wanted him to explain things like what the list was, where it came from, why I was on it – my mind was racing with dozens of unanswered questions, that's why I was so inarticulate.

Sir Humphrey tried to answer what he thought I was asking him.

'To put it absolutely bluntly, Minister, confidential investigations have revealed the existence of certain documents whose provenance is currently unestablished, but whose effect if realised would be to create a cabinet vacancy and precipitate a bye-election.'

I didn't know what he meant. I asked him.

'You are on a death list, Minister.'

We were going round in circles. 'Who . . . ?' I spluttered, 'What . . . ?'

'Ah,' he said. 'I see. It is the International Freedom Army. A new urban guerilla group, apparently.'

My bowels were turning to water. 'But what have they got against me?' I whispered.

Bernard reminded me of the vague rumours recently of a Cabinet reshuffle, and that my name has been mentioned in one or two of the papers in connection with the Ministry of Defence.

I asked who they could be, these urban guerillas. Bernard and Humphrey just shrugged.

'Hard to say, Minister. It could be an Irish splinter group, or Baader-Meinhof, or PLO, or Black September. It could be home-grown loonies – Anarchists, Maoists. Or it might be Libyans, Iranians, or the Italian Red Brigade for all we know.'

'In any case,' added Bernard, 'they're all interconnected really. This could simply be a new group of freelance killers. The Special Branch don't know where to start.'

That was *very* encouraging, I must say! I couldn't get over the cool, callous, unemotional way in which they were discussing some maniacs who were trying to kill me.

I tried to grasp at straws.

'There's a *list* of names, is there? You said a list? Not just me?'

'Not just you, Minister,' Sir Humphrey confirmed.

I said that I supposed that there were hundreds of names on it.

'Just three,' said Humphrey.

'Three?'

I was in a state of shock. I think. Or panic. One of those. I just sat there unable to think or speak. My mouth had completely dried up.

As I tried to say something, anything, the phone rang. Bernard answered it. Apparently somebody called Commander Forest from Special Branch had come to brief me.

Bernard went to get him. As he left he turned to me and said in a kindly fashion: 'Try looking at it this way, Minister – it's always nice to be on a shortlist. At least they know who you are.'

I gave him a withering look, and he hurried out.

Sir Humphrey filled in the background. The Special Branch had apparently informed the Home Secretary (the usual procedure) who recommended detectives to protect me.

I don't see how they can protect me. How can detectives protect me from an assassin's bullet? Nobody can. Everybody knows that.

I said this to Humphrey. I suppose I hoped he'd disagree – but he didn't. 'Look at it this way,' he responded. 'Even if detectives cannot protect anyone, they do ensure that the assassin is brought to justice. After the victim has been gunned down.'

Thanks a lot!

Bernard brought in Commander Forest. He was a tall thin cadaverous-looking individual, with a slightly nervous flinching manner. He didn't really inspire confidence.

I decided that I had to put on a brave show. Chin up, stiff upper lip, pull myself together, that sort of thing. I'd been talking a lot about leadership. Now I had to prove to them – and myself – that I was officer material.

I smiled reassuringly at the Commander, as he offered to brief me on the standard hazards and routine precautions. 'I don't really have to take these things too seriously, do I?' I asked in a cavalier manner.

'Well, sir, in a sense, it's up to you, but we do *advise* . . .'

I interrupted. 'Look, I can see that some people might get into a frightful funk but, well, it's the job, isn't it? All in a day's work.'

Commander Forest gazed at me strangely. 'I admire your courage, sir,' he said as if he really thought I were a raving idiot.

I decided I'd done enough of the stiff upper lip. I'd let him speak. 'Okay, shoot,' I said. It was an unfortunate turn of phrase.

'Read this,' he said, and thrust a Xeroxed typescript into my hand. 'This will tell you all you need to know. Study it, memorise it, and keep it to yourself.'

[*The Museum of the Metropolitan Police at New Scotland Yard has kindly lent us a copy of 'Security Precautions', the document handed to Hacker. It is self-explanatory – Ed.*]

SECURITY PRECAUTIONS

Assassination hazards fall broadly into four categories:
 i) BULLETS
 ii) BOMBS
 iii) POISONS
 iv) ACCIDENTS so-called
There is also the possibility of gassing, throttling, stabbing, drowning, garotting and ritual disembowelling, but most of these are comparatively infrequent in the UK

 i) BULLETS
  Snipers can be found in various locations
  (a) a high building
  (b) a car travelling beside your car
  (c) Stealing up close to you in a crowd
  (d) at your front door, as an unexpected caller
  (e) in a parked van, concealing a marksman
  (f) thrusting a revolver through your car window
    etc. etc.

  Precautions
  (a) Avoid crowds
  (b) Keep away from windows
    (Bullet-proof net curtains will be provided at your home and your office)
  (c) Never answer your own front door
  (d) Keep your car window up, windows and doors locked while you are driving
  (e) Never draw up at traffic lights on the pavement side
  (f) If a car pulls across in front of you, do *not* ram it in the middle. *Aim for one of the axles and sweep it aside*

    N.B. Initially, Special Branch Police Officers will not only answer your front door for you, but will give all available protection and cover: alarms, 24-hour patrols by your local constituency police force, special locks, phone taps, floodlights – etc

 ii) BOMBS
  (a) Car bombs – use regulation issue mirror at the end of a long pole, in order to check thoroughly the underside of your chassis each morning, and on any occasion on which the car has been left unattended

  (b) Letter/parcel bombs – never open any yourself
    N.B. For the time being all your mail will be redirected

 iii) POISON
  (a) *Gifts* of food and drink, chocolates, sweets, etc. – treat with suspicion
  (b) Check milk bottle tops in the morning for hyperdermic holes
  (c) Avoid strangers approaching you with umbrellas – (the ferrule jabbed in the calf/thigh method)

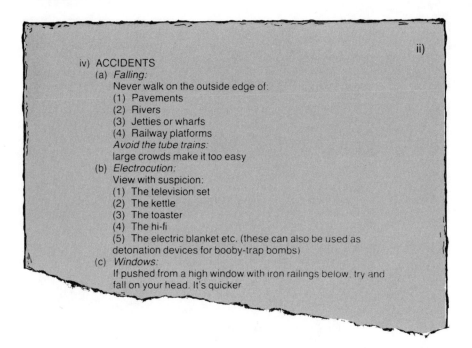

ii)

iv) ACCIDENTS
(a) *Falling:*
Never walk on the outside edge of:
(1) Pavements
(2) Rivers
(3) Jetties or wharfs
(4) Railway platforms
Avoid the tube trains:
large crowds make it too easy
(b) *Electrocution:*
View with suspicion:
(1) The television set
(2) The kettle
(3) The toaster
(4) The hi-fi
(5) The electric blanket etc. (these can also be used as detonation devices for booby-trap bombs)
(c) *Windows:*
If pushed from a high window with iron railings below. try and fall on your head. It's quicker

I read the document through. It seemed to me as though I had little chance of survival. But I must continue to have courage.

After Commander Forest had left, I asked Humphrey how the police would find these terrorists before they found me. That seems to be my only hope.

Sir Humphrey remarked that telephone tapping and electronic surveillance of all possible suspects is the best way of picking these bastards up.

'But,' he added cautiously, 'that does incur intolerable intrusion upon individual privacy.'

I carefully considered the implications of this comment.

And then I came to the conclusion. A slightly different conclusion, although I think that perhaps he had misunderstood what I'd been saying earlier.

I explained that, on the other hand, if the people's elected representatives are to represent the people, it follows that any attack on these elected representatives is, *in itself*, an attack on freedom and democracy. The reason is clear. Such threats strike at the very heart of the people's inalienable democratic right to be governed by the leaders of their choice. Therefore, the safety of these leaders must be protected by every possible means – however much we might regret the necessity for doing so or the measures that we may be forced to take.

I explained all this to Humphrey. He was in complete agreement – although I didn't care for his choice of words. 'Beautifully argued, Minister,' he replied. 'My view exactly – or else you're a dead duck.'

April 3rd

Today there was a slight embarrassment.

My petition arrived.

The petition against phone tapping and electronic surveillance, the one that I started a year and a half ago when I was in opposition and Editor of *Reform*. Bernard wheeled into the office a huge office trolley loaded with piles of exercise books and reams of paper. It now has two and a quarter million signatures. A triumph of organisation and commitment, and what the hell do I bloody well do with it?

It is now clear to me – now that I have the *full* facts which you cannot get when in opposition, of course – that surveillance is an indispensable weapon in the fight against organised terror and crime.

Bernard understood. He offered to file the petition.

I wasn't sure that filing it was the answer. We had acknowledged receipt from the deputation – they would never ask to see it again. And they would imagine that it was in safe hands since I'm the one who began it all.

I told him to shred it. 'Bernard,' I said, 'we must make certain that no one ever finds it again.'

'In that case,' replied Bernard, 'I'm sure it would be best to file it.'

[*This situation was not without precedent.*

In April 1965 the Home Secretary told the House of Commons that 'no useful purpose' would be served by re-opening the enquiry into the Timothy Evans case. This was despite a passionate appeal from a leading member of the Opposition front bench, Sir Frank Soskice, who said: 'My appeal to the Home Secretary is most earnest. I believe that if ever there was a debt due to justice and to the reputation both of our own judicial system and to the public conscience . . . that debt is one the Home Secretary should now repay.'

Interestingly enough, a general election had occurred between the launching and the presenting of the petition. Consequently the Home Secretary who rejected Sir Frank Soskice's impassioned appeal – and petition – for an enquiry was Sir Frank Soskice – Ed.]

April 11th

I've just had the most awful Easter weekend of my life.

Annie and I went off on our quiet little weekend together just like we used to.

Well – almost like we used to. Unfortunately, half the Special Branch came with us.

When we went for a quiet afternoon stroll through the woods, the whole place was swarming with rozzers.

They kept nice and close to us – very protective, but impossible for Annie and me to discuss anything but the weather. They all look the other way – *not*, I hasten to add, out of courtesy or respect for our privacy, but to see if they could spot any potential attacker leaping towards me over the primroses.

We went to a charming restaurant for lunch. It seemed as though the whole of Scotland Yard came too.

'How many for lunch?' asked the head waiter as we came in.

'Nine,' said Annie acidly. The weekend was not working out as she'd expected.

The head waiter offered us a nice table for two by the window, but it was vetoed by a sergeant. 'No, that's not safe,' he muttered to me, and turned to a colleague, 'we've chosen that table over there for the target.'

Target!

So Annie and I were escorted to a cramped little table in a poky little corner next to the kitchen doors. They banged open and shut right beside us, throughout our meal.

As we sat down I was briefed by one of the detectives. 'You sit here. Constable Ross will sit over there, watching the kitchen door – that's your escape route. We don't *expect* any assassins to be among the kitchen staff as we only booked in here late morning. I'll sit by the window. And if you do hear any gunshots, just dive under the table and I'll take care of it.'

I'm sure he meant to be reassuring.

I informed him that I wasn't a bit worried. Then I heard a loud report close to my head, and I crashed under the table.

An utterly humiliating experience – some seconds later I stuck my head out and realised that a champagne bottle had just been opened for the next table. I had to pretend that I'd just been practising.

By this time, with all this talk of escape routes, assassins in the kitchen and so forth, I'd gone right off my food. So had Annie. And our appetites weren't helped by overhearing one of the detectives at the next table order a spaghetti Bolognese followed by a T-bone steak with beans, peas, cauliflower and chips – and a bottle of Château Baron Philippe Rothschild 1961, no less!

He saw us staring at him, beamed, and explained that his job really took it out of him.

We stuck it for nearly two days. We went to the cinema on Saturday evening, but that made Annie even more furious. She'd wanted to see *La Cage aux Folles* but in the end we went to a James Bond film – I knew that none of the detectives liked foreign films, and it didn't seem fair to drag them along to a French film with subtitles.

Annie was black with rage because I'd put their choice first. When she put it like that, I saw what she meant. I hated the Bond film anyway – it was all about assassination attempts, and I couldn't stand it.

The detectives were very fed up with us when we walked out halfway through it.

Finally, back in our hotel, lying in the bed, rigid with tension, unable to go to the loo without being observed, followed and overheard, we heard the following murmured conversation outside the bedroom door.

'Are they going out again?'

'No, they've turned in for the night.'

'Is the target in there now?'

'Yeah – target's in bed with his wife.'

'They don't seem to be enjoying their holiday, do they?'

'No. Wonder why.'

We decided to get up and go home then and there.

But did we find peace and quiet? You bet we didn't. When we got to Birmingham at 1.45 a.m. on Sunday morning, the front garden was knee deep in the local bluebottles, all wanting to show that they were doing their bit. The flower beds were trampled underfoot, searchlights playing constantly on all sides of the house, Alsations baring their teeth and growling . . . Bedlam!

So now we lay in our *own* beds, still rigid with tension, still unable to go to the loo without some flat-foot examining it first, still with detectives knocking on the bedroom door and barging straight in while saying, 'May I just check your windows sir,' but with the additional pleasures of dogs barking and searchlights lighting up the whole room at intervals of twenty-nine seconds.

I told Annie, pathetically trying to make the best of it all, that she'd soon get used to being a famous man's wife. She didn't say anything. I think she'd almost rather be a famous man's widow.

Thank god we still weren't subject to surveillance.

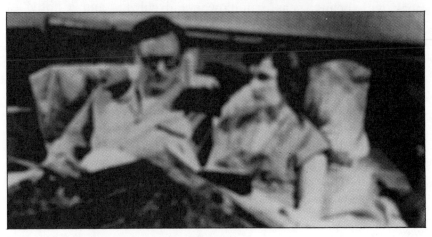

Secret photo released by the Special Branch at New Scotland Yard after the passing of the Freedom of Information Act, 1994

April 13th

Sunday I slept all day, since it's impossible to sleep at night.

Today I was back in the office and trying to handle a difficult interview with the dreadful Walter Fowler, who had somehow got wind of the petition. He seemed to find it extraordinary that I had now suppressed the petition that I started the year before last. Of course, he didn't know that my changed circumstances had made me see the whole matter of surveillance in a fresher and clearer way.

'I don't follow,' he complained. 'You say you're out to stop bugging and phone tapping. And now you get this petition. Two and a quarter million signatures. A terrific boost to your case. And you won't even give me a quote saying you welcome it?'

I made an unshakeable resolve to stay silent. Anything I said was liable to be quoted. You can't ever trust the press.

'What about making a promise to implement its main recommendations?'

I realised that I had to break my unshakeable resolve. 'Well you see Walter,' I began in most condescending manner, 'things aren't that simple.'

'Why not?' he asked.

'Security considerations,' I said.

'There always were,' he said. 'But you said yourself that "security" is the last excuse of a desperate bureaucrat.'

Irritating bastard. I resolved to stay silent again.

Then Walter said: 'Okay. I think I'll make it an even bigger story. MINISTER REJECTS HIS OWN PETITION.'

My resolve shook again. 'Steady on Walter,' I blurted out, 'don't be silly.'

'Are you accepting the petition or rejecting it?' he asked, giving me a simple choice.

'No,' I replied carefully.

Then it transpired that he *did* know all my circumstances. 'My Editor wants me to ask if being on the Freedom Army death list has altered your views in any way.'

Of course it has! Obviously! I'd be a complete fool if it hadn't.

'Certainly not,' I said. 'What an absurd idea! Never have occurred to me till you mentioned it just now.'

He didn't believe me but he couldn't prove anything. 'But how else am I to explain this sudden change of tune?'

I was getting a bit desperate by then, but thank God Bernard knocked on the door and appeared. Saved by the bell. He told me Humphrey wanted a word with me.

Humphrey came in. Walter didn't leave till I asked him if he minded. And he didn't leave the building – he just said he'd wait outside till we'd finished.

Humphrey asked me if I'd had a good weekend. Sadistic bastard. He must have known what my weekend would be like, with half the Special Branch present – all those romantic rozzers with the Smith and Wessons under their armpits.

He nodded sympathetically. 'The burdens of office,' he said.

'This can't go on!' I said. Why can't I keep my big mouth shut?

'I'm glad you said that,' he replied smoothly, 'because it isn't going to.' My jaw dropped open. 'We've just heard from the Special Branch that your protection is being withdrawn.'

Withdrawn? I was appalled. I thought he'd misunderstood me. I asked why?

'The police have suffered an acute personnel establishment short-fall.'

I was about to ask if anybody was hurt, when I realised what he meant. Short staffed. He meant short staffed! And because the police were short staffed they were going to allow me to be killed? I was horrified.

'There is a much more real and dangerous threat to the Soviet Premier at the Chequers meeting tomorrow,' he continued.

Much more real and dangerous? More real and dangerous to *him*, maybe. I searched desperately for an argument for them to protect me rather than him. 'He's Russian,' I said. 'I'm British!'

Then Sir Humphrey revealed further reasons why my protection was to be withdrawn.

'In fact, Minister, the Special Branch are confident that the threat to your life has diminished.'

Naturally I was anxious to know how they could be so bloody confident.

'Surveillance, Minister. They overheard a conversation.' Humphrey seemed reluctant to tell me. I told him to spit it out, that I had a right to know, and that I wanted a straight answer!

He nodded, and then went into his normal mumbo-jumbo. God knows what he said, I couldn't unravel it.

SIR BERNARD WOOLLEY RECALLS:[1]
I recall what Sir Humphrey said because I minuted it at the time. He explained that in view of the somewhat nebulous and inexplicit nature of Hacker's remit and the arguably marginal and peripheral nature of Hacker's influence on the central deliberations and decisions within the political process, there would be a case for restructuring their action priorities in such a way as to eliminate Hacker's liquidation from their immediate agenda.

[*Hacker's diary continues – Ed.*]

So I asked him to put it into English. He then said that the Freedom Army had apparently decided that I wasn't really important enough for it to be worth assassinating me.

He put it as gently as he could, I could see that. Even so, it was a bit of a blow. Not that they'd decided not to assassinate me, of course, but a bit of a blow to my pride nonetheless.

I asked Humphrey what he thought of this new situation. 'I don't agree with them, of course,' he said.

'You mean,' I asked, 'you think I *should* be assassinated?'

'No, no.'

'You mean, I'm not important enough?'

'No-oo – I mean you *are* important enough but they shouldn't assassinate you anyway.' He breathed a sigh of relief.

Anyway, it seemed I was off the hook, and perhaps that's all to the good. I mean, there's no point in being important but dead, is

[1] In conversation with the Editors.

there? But, if terrorist loonies even doubt my value to the government there's clearly some image-building repairs to be done right away.

Bernard then asked me if I'd finish my interview with Walter Fowler. Of course, I was delighted to.

He was ushered in, and I opened up right away. I told Bernard to bring the petition along on the trolley, so that Walter could see how big it was.

Bernard said, 'The petition? But I thought you said . . .'

'Yes I did,' I interrupted hastily. 'Could you get it Bernard?' He still looked blank. 'Antennae, Bernard,' I explained.

The penny dropped. 'Ah. Yes. Indeed, Minister,' he said quickly. 'You mean, I'm to get the petition that you said you were so pleased with?'

The boy's learning.

Walter demanded an answer to his various questions. I told him to sit down. Then I told him that I welcomed the petition, warmly. That it is not just something you sweep under the carpet.

Bernard Woolley receiving the petition and wondering how to sweep it under the carpet (DAA Archives)

'And as for death lists,' I concluded. 'Well – Ministers are dispensable, but freedom is indivisible. Isn't that so, Humphrey?'

'Yes Minister,' replied my smiling Permanent Secretary, dead on cue.

4

The Greasy Pole

[*There are times in a politician's life when he is obliged to take the wrong decision. Wrong economically, wrong industrially, wrong by any standards – except one. It is a curious fact that something which is wrong from every other point of view can be right politically. And something which is right politically does not simply mean that it's the way to get the votes – which it is – but also, if a policy gets the votes then it can be argued that that policy is what the people want. And, in a democracy, how can a thing be wrong if it is what the people will vote for?*

The incident in question only came to light slowly. The first reference that we can find to it is not in Jim Hacker's diary, but in Steel Yourself, *the memoirs of that uniquely outspoken Chairman of the British Chemical Corporation the diminutive Glaswegian industrialist and scientist, Sir Wally McFarland.*

McFarland was known for his plain language and his unwillingness to bow to government interference in his nationalised industry. He was an expert both on chemicals and on business management – and he believed (rightly) that Hacker knew little or nothing about either. His low regard for Hacker was matched only by his contempt for Sir Humphrey's skill in business. Like many businessmen, he believed that in commerce the Civil Service was not safe with a whelk stall – Ed.]

From Steel Yourself:

On 16 April I had a meeting with Sir Humphrey Appleby at the Department of Administrative Affairs. It was the umpteenth meeting on the subject of the manufacture of Propanol on Merseyside under licence from the Italian Government.

To my astonishment Sir Humphrey seemed to indicate that there might be a problem with the Minister, but his language was as opaque as usual and I could not be sure of this.

I asked him if he was havering. [*Scottish word, meaning to be indecisive – Ed.*] He denied it, but said that we cannot take the Minister's approval for granted.

This was and still is incomprehensible to me. The Italian government was offering us a massive contract to manufacture Propanol at our Merseyside plant. This contract meant saving a plant which we would otherwise have to close down. It meant taking people on, instead of laying them off. And it meant big export royalties. We'd been fighting for two years to win it against tough German and US competition. It seemed completely obvious that it *had* to go ahead.

Appleby raised some footling idiotic question about what the Minister might think. In my experience Ministers *don't* think. In my ten years as Chairman of the BCC I dealt with nineteen different Ministers. They never stopped to think, even if they possessed the basic intelligence necessary for thought – which several of them did not. As a matter of fact, they were usually too lazy to talk to me because they were usually talking to the trade union leaders and bribing them not to strike.

I told Appleby my views. He denied that trade union leaders were bribed. Naturally. It may not be technically bribery, but what else do you call conversations that amount to 'Have a quango, Tom. Have a knighthood, Dick. Have a peerage, Harry'?

Appleby said that the Minister was worried about the Propanol scheme. If so, why hadn't anything been said till now?

At this stage I – unwisely, perhaps – brushed aside suggestions that the Minister was worried. He'd never shown any real interest in the scheme, so he could know nothing about it. Naïvely, I assumed that his ignorance would prevent him interfering. And, in any case, all Ministers are worried. I never met a Minister who wasn't worried.

Ministers worry whenever you do anything that is bold. Anything that makes business sense. Anything that is *necessary*, in fact. If I had never done anything to worry any of those lily-livered, vote-grubbing, baby-kissing jellies the BCC would have gone down the tube ten years earlier than it did.

Appleby said that the Minister's worries centred on the fact that Propanol contained metadioxin. [*Dioxin was the chemical released in the accident at Seveso, Italy, some years earlier. It was believed to cause damage to the foetus – Ed.*] This was typical. Metadioxin is completely different, an inert compound. It had a clean bill of health from the FDA [*Food and Drugs Administration – Ed.*] in Washington. And the Henderson Committee was about to approve it.

Nonetheless, I could see that Appleby, in all his ignorance of chemistry, was still a little worried. Or else he was reflecting Hacker's worries.

I added that the name metadioxin was now not in the proposal. The chemical was simply called Propanol, making it politically safe.

Our meeting concluded with Appleby offering assurances that the Minister was unlikely to raise any objections, as long as the matter was handled with tact. I offered to go along myself, and have a tactful word with Hacker, and persuade that egotistical blancmange that there was no argument on the matter.

Appleby declined my offer, and answered that he would be able to manage without what he generously called my unique and refreshing brand of tact.

I was not so sure. And, again, I was locked out of the crucial meeting.

Why do governments continually hire experts to run nationalised industries on business lines, and then interfere every time you try to make a business decision?

[*Hacker's diary continues – Ed.*]

April 16th

This morning Humphrey gave me some wonderful news. Or what appeared to be wonderful news.

He handed me a paper which summarised a new industrial scheme for Merseyside. In a nutshell, the plan is to turn a run-down chemical plant into one of the most profitable units in the British Chemical Corporation. Overnight it will make the BCC into the largest manufacturer of Propanol in Europe.

The benefits would be immense: capital equipment to be made in British factories, additional rateable income for the Local Authority, new jobs on Merseyside, foreign exchange from the exports, it all seemed too good to be true.

I said so.

'But it *is* true, Minister,' said Sir Humphrey, beaming.

How could it be, I asked myself. *Then* I asked myself, what's the point of asking myself? So I asked Humphrey.

'How could it be?' I asked. 'What's the snag?'

'The snag?' repeated Humphrey.

'Yes,' I repeated. 'The snag. What is the snag?'

I knew there must be some snag.

'I don't think I quite follow what you mean, precisely?' Humphrey was playing for time, I could tell.

I formulated my worries even as I voiced them. 'Well . . . what I mean is, this Propanol stuff is an Italian product. So why don't they produce it in Italy?' Humphrey was silent. This was indeed suspicious. 'Why are they making us such a generous present?'

'There's no snag about this, Minister,' said Sir Humphrey. 'It's wonderful news.'

I could see that if it *were* wonderful news, it would indeed be wonderful news.

'Yes,' I agreed cautiously. 'It *is* wonderful news. Wonderful news, isn't it?' I said to Bernard, who was taking the minutes on my right.

He flashed a glance at Humphrey, then replied warily, 'Yes, wonderful news,' but he didn't sound at all carefree.

I knew I'd find out nothing more, just by asking in a generalised fashion about snags. So I thought hard, I tried to find the right question. Humphrey would never actually lie to me. [*Well, hardly ever – Ed.*] and will give me the right answers if I can only think of the right questions.

'Good old Propanol,' I said playing for time. Then, quite suddenly, it came to me. 'What *is* Propanol?' I asked.

'It's rather interesting,' said Humphrey promptly. 'It used to be made with dioxin, until the Seveso explosion in Northern Italy. Then they had to stop making it. Now they've developed a safe compound called metadioxin, but of course the Italian factory is still sealed off. So they've asked the BCC to make it for them.'

'Ah,' the fog was beginning to lift. 'An ill wind, eh?'

'Quite so,' he agreed contentedly.

'But is this new stuff perfectly safe?'

'Perfectly,' he replied.

'Good,' I said. So I was no nearer. Or was I?

'Humphrey, are you givng me a categorical and absolute assurance that this stuff is not only safe, but one hundred per cent safe?'

'Yes, Minister.'

Okay, so what's up? Why do I smell danger somewhere in all this unequivocally good news? 'Have you anything else to add, Humphrey, which you might regret later if you don't say it now?'

'Well Minister, I suppose I should point out that some weak Ministers might have doubts, in view of the similarity of the names, but no one with any backbone would be deflected from such a beneficial project on such a flimsy pretext.'

So that's all that it was. The similarity of the names. Humphrey was right. I told him so in the most forthright terms. 'Absolutely! I know the sort of Minister you mean. Political jellyfish. Frightened of taking any decision that might upset someone. After all, every decision upsets *someone*. Government is about doing what's right, not doing what's popular. Eh, Humphrey?'

Humphrey was full of approval. 'I couldn't have expressed it better myself, Minister.' Conceited bugger. 'I'll tell Sir Wally to go ahead.'

This sounded a touch more hurried than usual. I stopped Humphrey as he walked to the door, and sought further reassurance.

'Um . . . this decision *will* be popular, though, won't it?'

'Very popular,' Humphrey replied firmly.

I *still* felt a certain nagging worry, somewhere in my bones. 'Humphrey, I just want to be clear on this. You're not asking me to take a courageous decision, are you?'

Humphrey was visibly shocked. 'Of *course* not, Minister,' he insisted. 'Not even a controversial one. What a suggestion!'

[*Readers of Volume One of Hacker's Diaries will doubtless recall that whereas a controversial decision will merely lose you votes, a courageous decision will lose you the election – Ed.*]

Nonetheless, if I let it go at this, if anything went wrong I knew I should have to carry the can. So I suggested that perhaps we might take this matter to Cabinet.

'In my opinion,' Humphrey answered revealingly, 'the less said about this the better.'

'Why?'

'Because,' he said patiently, 'although metadioxin is totally harmless, the name might cause anxiety in ignorant and prejudiced minds.'

I was about to tick him off for referring to my Cabinet colleagues in this way (right though he was!) when I realised that he was referring to Friends of the Earth and other pressure groups.

April 18th

The matter of the Propanol plant is still not fully agreed. Joan Littler, MP for Liverpool South West, came to see me today.

I didn't even know she was coming. I checked with Bernard, who reminded me that not only is she the PM's PPS [*Parliamentary Private Secretary, the first – and unpaid – rung on the government ladder – Ed.*] but also that the new Propanol plant would be in her constituency.

I told Bernard to bring her in. To my surprise (well, not *quite* to my surprise) Humphrey appeared at the door and asked if he could join us.

She came in, and I introduced her to Humphrey. She's in her late thirties, quite attractive in a pulled-through-a-hedge-backwards Shirley Williams' sort of way, and her slightly soft feminine manner disguises a hard-nosed opportunist. And she has the PM's ear, of course.

There was something rather aggressive about her opening gambit.

'Look here Jim, what's the British Chemical Corporation up to in my constituency?'

'Well . . .' I began.

Sir Humphrey interrupted. 'They will shortly be announcing a very exciting project involving new jobs and new investment.'

She nodded, and turned to me. 'Yes, but there are some very worrying rumours about this project.'

'Such as?' I enquired in my most helpful tone.

She eyed me carefully. 'Rumours about dangerous chemicals.'

I nodded. 'Yes, well,' I began, 'obviously all chemicals have some element of danger . . .'

Humphrey interrupted again. 'The Minister means that the rumours are completely unfounded and there is no cause for alarm.'

I nodded. It was a good reply.

She didn't seem to think so. 'All the same,' she persisted, 'can I have your assurance, Jim, that first of all there'll be a full public enquiry?'

This seemed, I must say, a perfectly reasonable request. 'Actually,' I began, 'there'd be no harm in having a public enquiry, it might be . . .'

Humphrey interjected. 'The Minister was about to say that there is absolutely no need for a public enquiry. The whole matter has been fully investigated already and a report will be published shortly.'

Humphrey, it seemed to me, was being a little high-handed. Clearly Joan thought so too.

'Listen,' she said forcefully, 'I came here to talk to Jim.'

And Humphrey, as charming as ever replied, 'and indeed you are talking to him.'

'But he's not answering! You are!'

I could quite see her point. Humphrey's helpfulness will sometimes achieve the opposite effect from what it was designed to achieve. Unfortunately, he was insensitive to this.

'The Minister and I,' continued Sir Humphrey complacently, 'are of one mind.'

She was incensed. 'Whose mind? Your mind?' She turned on me. 'Listen, I've heard on the grapevine that this factory will be making the chemical that poisoned Seveso and the whole of Northern Italy.'

'That's not true,' I replied, before Humphrey could screw things up further. I explained that the chemical in Seveso was dioxin, whereas this is metadioxin.

'But,' she asserted, 'that must be virtually the same thing.'

I assured her that it was merely a similar name.

'But,' she insisted, 'it's the same name, with "meta" stuck on the front.'

'Ah yes,' I agreed, 'but that makes all the difference.'

'Why?' she asked. 'What does meta mean?'

Of course, I hadn't the slightest idea. So I was forced to ask Humphrey.

'Simple, Minister,' he explained. 'It means "with" or "after", or sometimes "beyond" – it's from the Greek, you know.'

[*Like all Permanent Secretaries, Sir Humphrey Appleby was a generalist. Most of them studied classics, history, PPE or modern languages. Of course you might expect the Permanent Secretary at the Department of Administrative Affairs to have a degree in business administration, but of course you would be wrong – Ed.*]

Then he went on to explain that metadioxin means 'with' or 'after' dioxin, depending on whether it's with the accusative or the genitive: with the accusative it's 'beyond' or 'after', with the genitive it's 'with' – as in Latin, where the ablative is used for words needing a sense of with to precede them.

Bernard added – speaking for the first time in the whole meeting – that of course there is no ablative in Greek, as I would doubtless recall.

I told him I recalled no such thing, and later today he wrote me a little memo, explaining all the above Greek and Latin grammar.

However, I hoped these explanations would satisfy Joan Littler. And that, like me, she would be unwilling to reveal the limits of her education. No such luck.

'I still don't understand,' she said disarmingly.

Humphrey tried snobbery. 'Oh dear,' he sighed 'I should have thought that was perfectly clear.' It never works.

Her eyes flashed. 'What I insist on knowing,' she stated, 'is what is the actual difference between dioxin and metadioxin.'

I didn't know, of course. Humphrey sailed into the rescue. 'It's very simple,' he replied grandly. 'Metadioxin is an inert compound of dioxin.'

I hoped that that would be that. But no.

She looked at me for help. I, of course, was unable to give her any. So I looked at Humphrey.

'Um, Humphrey,' I said, bluffing madly, 'I *think* I follow that but, er, could you, er just explain that a little more clearly?'

He stared at me, coldly. 'In what sense, Minister?'

I didn't know where to start. I was going to have to think of the right question again. But Joan said: 'What does inert mean?'

Sir Humphrey stared at her, silently. And in that glorious moment I suddenly realised that he had no idea what he was talking about either.

'Well,' he said eventually, 'inert means that . . . it's not . . . ert.'

We all stared at each other in silence.

'Ah,' said Joan Littler.

'Ah,' I said.

'Wouldn't 'ert a fly,' muttered Bernard. At least, I think that's what he said, but when I asked him to repeat it he refused and fell silent.

And again, Joan Littler persisted.

'But,' she pressed me, 'what does that mean in practical terms?'

'You mean, chemically?' I asked her. My degree is in economics.

'Yes, chemically,' she said.

Again, I turned to Humphrey. 'Yes,' I said, beginning to enjoy myself, 'what does it mean chemically, Humphrey?'

His eyes spun. Bluffing magnificently, he said in his most patronising voice. 'Well, I'm not sure that I can explain in layman's language, Minister.'

I called the bluff. 'Do you know *any* chemistry, Humphrey?' I enquired.

'Of course not, Minister. I was in the Scholarship form.'

[*At any English public school – 'public' meaning 'private', of course – the scholarship form would have meant the classics form. Indeed, if you went to a very good school indeed you might avoid learning any science at all – Ed.*]

'And while we're at it,' continued Joan Littler, 'what's a compound?'

'You don't know any chemistry either?'

'No,' she replied. 'Do you?'

Suddenly, this all seemed awfully funny. None of us knew *anything* about the matter we were discussing. Joan, Humphrey, Bernard and I, all charged with a vital decision on a matter of government policy – and you couldn't have found four people anywhere in the UK who understood less about it.

[*It is significant that none of those present thought of telephoning Sir Wally McFarland. But then, he was merely the expert, and the chairman of the Nationalised Industry in question – Ed.*]

I grinned, embarrassed, like a naughty schoolboy. 'We *ought* to know something about inert compounds, oughtn't we?'

Humphrey had no sense of humour about this, and he made a brave attempt at bluffing us again.

'A compound is . . . well, you know what compound interest is, surely?' he complained. Joan and I nodded. 'Compound interest is a jolly good thing to enjoy. Well, that's the sort of thing a compound is.'

I stared at him. Did he really think that would do? I looked at Joan. She was staring at him too. But reduced to silence for the first time. So I plunged in hopefully.

'Well,' I said, trying it on in the hope of bringing the discussion to a close, 'that's about it, then. To sum up, I think we're all of the same mind basically in agreement, broadly speaking, about this. And we are happy to continue with its development.'

Littler spoke up. 'I've said no such thing.'

We were getting nowhere. So I tried to sum it up again. I pointed out that we had established that the only similarity between dioxin and metadioxin was in the name. She didn't seem to see it.

I searched desperately for an analogy, 'It's like Littler and Hitler,' I explained. 'We're not saying that you're like Hitler because your name sounds similar.'

I realised that I'd been less than tactful, but the words were out. She flared up. 'That's not the point,' she said angrily.

'Then what *is* the point?' But I knew already.

'The point is, that this factory is in my constituency.'

Of course I could see why she was worried, but if Humphrey was telling me the truth she was worried unnecessarily. 'It's good for the constituency.' I said. 'More jobs. More money. The only people who could possibly be upset by this are a few cranky environmentalists. It can't cost us more than, on balance, a couple of hundred votes.'

'My majority,' she replied quietly, 'is ninety-one.'

I hadn't realised. She certainly had a point. I don't want to be responsible for jeopardising a government-held marginal, especially if the sitting MP is PPS to the PM.

She pressed home her argument. 'And don't forget that there are three government constituencies bordering onto mine – all marginal, all with majorities of well under two thousand.'

I didn't know what to say. While I considered the position, Sir Humphrey spoke up again. 'Miss Littler,' he began, 'may I intervene once more?' She nodded. 'The case for the BCC manufacturing Propanol is overwhelming – am I right, Minister?'

'Overwhelming,' I agreed.

'It will create jobs,' continued Humphrey fluently, 'it will increase income for the Local Authority, and it will secure profitable export orders.'

'Export orders,' I agreed.

'Furthermore,' he continued, 'the chemical has been declared safe by the FDA in Washington.'

'Washington,' I agreed.

'We are having,' he went on,' a report prepared here *as well*. The Minister regards this scheme as being wholly to the advantage of your constituency and the country.'

I chimed in. 'And if the stuff is dangerous, I *pro. nise* you I'll stop it being made here. But if the report shows it's harmless, that would be absurd, wouldn't it?'

She sat still for a moment, staring at me, then at Humphrey. Then she stood up. She said she wasn't satisfied. (I can't blame her. If it were my constituency, I'm not sure I'd be satisfied either.) She advised me to remember that the Party made me an MP – and that I certainly can't go on being a Minister if our party loses the next election.

She's got a point there too.

Also, I have a nasty feeling that the PM will hear her point of view before the end of the week.

Humphrey looked at me after she left, obviously asking for a go-ahead. I told him that I would consider the matter further, and told Bernard to put all the relevant papers in my box to take home and study. Then the decision should become clear.

April 18th

I've studied all the Propanol papers and I still don't know what to do.

So I called a meeting with Humphrey to discuss the report on Propanol that we have commissioned. I've been wondering if it really will be conclusively in favour of Propanol, as Sir Humphrey and Sir Wally predict.

I asked if I should meet Professor Henderson, who is chairing the report, or writing it himself or something.

Humphrey said that there was no need for such a meeting. He is apparently a brilliant bio-chemist and was chosen with some care.

Naturally he was chosen with care. But to what end: to produce a report that backs Sir Wally and Sir Humphrey? Naturally he was.

But surely none of them would be foolish enough to cook up a report saying that metadioxin were safe if, in fact, it were dangerous. Naturally not. I think I'm going round in circles.

There was another possibility that I could raise though. 'Suppose he produces one of those cautious wait-and-see reports?'

'In that case,' said Sir Humphrey cheerfully, 'we don't publish it, we use the American report instead.'

I was completely torn. On the one hand, the scheme is a wonderful one – the jobs, the income etc. – if it works out safely! And I'm assured it will. But if there's an accident after I have given the go-ahead . . . The consequences would be too awful to contemplate.

'Is there any chance he'll produce a report saying the stuff's dangerous?' I wanted to know.

Humphrey was plainly baffled. 'No. No chance. It isn't dangerous,' he said.

He clearly is totally sincere on this issue. And yet he's suggesting we don't publish a cautious wait-and-see type report if that's what Henderson writes.

'Why would you consider suppressing the Henderson report?'

He was outraged. 'I would never suppress it, Minister. I merely might not publish it.'

'What's the difference?'

'All the difference in the world. Suppression is the instrument of totalitarian dictatorships. You can't do that in a free country. We would merely take a democratic decision not to publish it.'

That makes sense. But what would I say to the press and to Parliament, I wondered? That we had hoped the Henderson Committee would show we'd made the right decision but instead they've said we cocked it up, so we're pretending the report doesn't exist? I offered this suggestion to Humphrey.

He was not amused. 'Very droll, Minister,' he remarked.

So I asked Humphrey, 'What *would* I say, if I decided not to publish it?'

'There is a well-established government procedure for suppressing – that is, not publishing – unwanted reports.'

This was news to me. I asked how it was done.

'You discredit them,' he explained simply.

How? I made notes as he spoke. It occurred to me, that his technique could be useful for discrediting some of the party's more idiotic research papers.

Stage one: The public interest
1) You hint at security considerations.

2) You point out that the report could be used to put unwelcome press-ure on government because it might be misinterpreted. [*Of course, anything might be misinterpreted. The Sermon on the Mount might be misinterpreted. Indeed, Sir Humphrey Appleby would almost certainly have argued that, had the Sermon on the Mount been a government report, it should certainly not have been published on the grounds that it was a thoroughly irresponsible document: the sub-paragraph suggest-ing that the meek will inherit the earth could, for instance, do irreparable damage to the defence budget – Ed.*]

3) You then say that it is better to wait for the results of a wider and more detailed survey over a longer time-scale.

4) If there is no such survey being carried out, so much the better. You commission one, which gives you even more time to play with.

Stage two: Discredit the evidence that you are not publishing
This is, of course, much easier than discrediting evidence that you *do* publish. You do it indirectly, by press leaks. You say:
  (a) that it leaves important questions unanswered
  (b) that much of the evidence is inconclusive
  (c) that the figures are open to other interpretations
  (d) that certain findings are contradictory
  (e) that some of the main conclusions have been questioned
Points (a) to (d) are bound to be true. In fact, all of these criticisms can be made of a report without even reading it. There are for instance, always *some* questions unanswered – such as the ones they haven't asked. As regards (e), if some of the main conclusions have not been questioned, question them! Then they have.

Stage three: Undermine the recommendations
This is easily done, with an assortment of governmental phrases:
  (a) 'not really a basis for long term decisions . . .'
  (b) 'not sufficient information on which to base a valid assess-ment . . .'
  (c) 'no reason for any fundamental rethink of existing policy . . .'
  (d) 'broadly speaking, it endorses current practice . . .'
These phrases give comfort to people who have not read the report and who don't want change – i.e. almost everybody.

Stage four: If stage three still leaves doubts, then Discredit The Man Who Produced the Report
This must be done OFF THE RECORD. You explain that:
  (a) he is harbouring a grudge against the government
  (b) he is a publicity seeker
  (c) he's trying to get his knighthood
  (d) he is trying to get his chair
  (e) he is trying to get his Vice-Chancellorship
  (f) he used to be a consultant to a multi-national company *or*
  (g) he wants to be a consultant to a multi-national company

April 19th
Today the Propanol plan reached the television news, damn it. Somehow some environmental group got wind of the scheme and a row blew up on Merseyside.

The TV newsreader – or whoever writes what the newsreader reads – didn't help much either. Though he didn't say that Propanol was dangerous, he somehow managed to imply it – using loaded words like 'claim'.

[*We have found the transcript of the BBC 9 O'Clock News for April 17th. The relevant item is shown overleaf. Hacker seems to have a reasonable point – Ed.*]

BRITISH BROADCASTING CORPORATION

NEWSREADER: Apparently Propanol contains metadioxin, which the BCC claims is completely harmless. It is, however, a compound of dioxin, which was the chemical released

CUE NEWS FILM OF SEVESO INCIDENT

after a factory explosion at Seveso in Northern Italy in July 1976, spreading a cloud of poisonous dust over a four mile radius. Because dioxin can cause irreversible damage to the human foetus as well as other serious diseases the entire village was evacuated and the villagers were not allowed to return home for nearly a year.

CUE FILM OF MERSEYSIDE PROTEST.   Group of women with placards: "NO TO THE POISON FACTORY", "BABYKILLERS KEEP OUT", "LIVES BEFORE PROFITS".

Today a Merseyside group of protesters voice their opposition to the BCC scheme outside the factory gates.

LIVERPOOL WOMAN: I'll tell you what we're going to do. As far as I'm concerned, Sir Wally can take his poisonous chemicals somewhere else. My daughter's expecting a baby in three months and I'm not having my grandchild deformed for the sake of blood Eyties[1] I can tell you that.

REPORTER: But they say metadioxin is harmless.

LIVERPOOL WOMAN: Oh yes. They said Thalidomide was harmless too, didn't they? Well if it's all that harmless, why aren't they Eyties making it in Italy, eh? Tell me that! If we had a government that cared about ordinary people, they'd never allow it.

END OF FILM

NEWSREADER: The BCC said tonight that a Government Report on the safety of Propanol was due to be published shortly by the Department of Administrative Affairs. Today, in Prague, the Government announced that due to ....

- 1 -

---

[1] Italians.

[We asked an old BBC current affairs man how the News would have treated the item if they had been in favour of the scheme, and we reproduce his 'favourable' version to compare with the actual one – Ed.]

NEWSREADER: Propanol contains metadioxin, a compound of the chemical dioxin which was released in the Seveso explosion in Italy in 1976. It is however an inert compound and chemical analysis has shown it to be completely harmless.

CUT TO FILM OF FACTORY SHOWING PLANT AND OFFICES

The news was welcomed today at the factory where Propanol will be manufactured. It had been scheduled for closure at the end of the year, but now it will be taking on more staff. The contract is for a minimum of five years.

CUE FILM OF FACTORY WORKER

FACTORY WORKER: This is great news. At last we've got some work we can get our teeth into. It's really put heart in the lads.

CUT TO SIR WALLY

SIR WALLY: Everyone's worked like mad for this contract. It will mean a lot of exports as well as a lot of jobs. We were up against the Germans and the Americans, so it's a real vote of confidence in the British chemical industry.

REPORTER: Isn't metadioxin potentially dangerous?

SIR WALLY: No, that's dioxin; metadioxin is about as dangerous as self-raising flour.

END OF FILM

NEWSREADER: A government report is to be published shortly which, it is understood, will confirm an earlier American enquiry which gives metadioxin a clean bill of health.

April 20th

I summoned Humphrey first thing this morning. I pointed out that metadioxin is dynamite.

He answered me that it's harmless.

I disagreed. 'It may be harmless chemically,' I said, 'but not politically.'

'It can't hurt anyone,' he insisted.

I pointed out that it could finish me off.

No sooner had we begun talking than Number Ten was on the phone. The political office. Joan Littler had obviously made sure that Number Ten watched the Nine O'Clock News last night.

I tried to explain that this was merely a little local difficulty, and there were exports and jobs prospects. They asked how many jobs: I had to admit that it was only about ninety – but well-paid jobs, and in an area of high unemployment.

None of this cut any ice with Number Ten – I was talking to the Chief Political Advisor, but doubtless he was acting under orders. There was no point in fighting this particular losing battle with the PM, so I muttered (as Humphrey was listening, and Bernard was probably listening-in) that I was coming round to their point of view *i.e.* that there was a risk to three or four marginals.

I rang off. Humphrey was eyeing me with a quizzical air.

'Humphrey,' I began carefully, 'something has just struck me.'

'I noticed,' he replied dryly.

I ignored the wise-crack. I pointed out that there were perfectly legitimate arguments against this scheme. A loss of public confidence, for instance.

'You mean votes,' he interjected.

I denied it, of course. I explained that I didn't exactly mean votes. Votes in themselves are not a consideration. But *the public will* is a valid consideration. We are a democracy. And it looks as if the public are against this scheme.

'The public,' said Sir Humphrey, 'are ignorant and misguided.'

'What do you mean?' I demanded. 'It was the public who elected me.'

There was a pointed silence.

Then Sir Humphrey continued: 'Minister, in a week it will all have blown over, and in a year's time there will be a safe and successful factory on Merseyside.'

'A week is a long time in politics,' I answered.[1]

[1] Originally said by Mr Harold Wilson as he then was.

'A year is a short time in government,' responded Sir Humphrey.

I began to get cross. *He* may be in government. But I'm in politics. And the PM is not pleased.

Humphrey then tried to tell me that I was putting party before country. That hoary old cliché again. I told him to find a new one.

Bernard said that a new cliché could perhaps be said to be a contradiction in terms. Thank you, Bernard, for all your help!

I made one more attempt to make Humphrey understand. 'Humphrey,' I said, 'you understand nothing because you lead a sheltered life. I want to survive. I'm not crossing the PM.'

He was very bitter. And very insulting. 'Must you always be so concerned with climbing the greasy pole?'

I faced the question head on. 'Humphrey,' I explained, 'the greasy pole is important. I have to climb it.'

'Why?'

'Because,' I said, 'it's there.'

April 21st
Today there was an astonishing piece in *The Times*. A leak.

HENDERSON REPORT CLEARS PROPANOL

I was furious.

I asked Bernard how *The Times* knows the wording of the Henderson Report before I do.

'There's been a leak, Minister,' he explained.

The boy's a fool. Obviously there's been a leak. The question is, who's been leaking?

On second thoughts, perhaps he's not a fool. Perhaps he knows. And can't or won't tell.

'It's labelled "Confidential",' I pointed out.

'At least it wasn't labelled "Restricted",' he said.

[*RESTRICTED means it was in the papers yesterday. CONFIDENTIAL means it won't be in the papers till today – Ed.*]

I decided to put Bernard on the spot. 'Who leaked this? Humphrey?'

'Oh,' he said. 'I'm sure he didn't.'

'Are you?' I asked penetratingly.

'Well . . . he probably didn't.'

'No?' I was at my most penetrating.

'Well,' said Bernard with a sheepish smile, 'it *might* have been someone else.'

'These leaks are a disgrace,' I told him. 'And people think that it's politicians that leak.'

'It has been known, though, hasn't it?' said Bernard carefully.

'In my opinion,' I said reproachfully, 'we are much more leaked against than leaking.'

I then read *The Times* story carefully through. It contained a number of phrases that I could almost hear Humphrey dictating: 'Political cowardice to reject the BCC proposal' . . . 'Hacker has no choice', etc.

It was clear that, by means of this leak, Humphrey thinks that he has now committed me to this scheme.

Well, we shall see!

April 22nd

I got my copy of the Henderson Report, only a day after *The Times* got theirs. Not bad.

The Report gives me no way out of the Propanol scheme. At least, none that I can see at the moment. It says it's a completely safe chemical.

On the other hand, *The Times* commits me to nothing. It is, after all, merely an unofficial leak of a draft report.

Sir Wally McFarlane was my first appointment of the day. Humphrey came too – surprise, surprise!

And they were both looking excessively cheerful.

I asked them to sit down. Then Sir Wally opened the batting.

'I see from the press,' he said, 'that the Henderson Report comes down clearly on our side.'

I think perhaps he still thinks that I'm on his side. No, surely Humphrey must have briefed him. So he's pretending that he thinks that I'm still on his side.

I was non-committal. 'Yes, I saw that too.'

And I stared penetratingly at Humphrey.

He shifted uncomfortably in his seat. 'Yes, that committee is leaking like a sieve.' I continued staring at him, but made no reply. There's no doubt that he's the guilty man. He continued, brazenly: 'So Minister, there's no real case for refusing permission for the new

Plant now, is there?'

I remained non-committal. 'I don't know.'

Sir Wally spoke up. 'Look, Jim. We've been working away at this contract for two years. It's very important to us. I'm chairman and I'm responsible – and I tell you, as a chemist myself, that metadioxin is utterly safe.'

'Why do you experts always think you are right?' I enquired coldly.

'Why do you think,' countered Sir Wally emotionally, 'that the more *in*expert you are, the more likely *you* are to be right?'

I'm not an expert. I've never claimed to be an expert. I said so. 'Ministers are not experts. Ministers are put in charge precisely because they know nothing . . .'

'You admit that?' interrupted Sir Wally with glee. I suppose I walked right into that.

I persevered. 'Ministers know nothing *about technical problems*. A Minister's job is to consider the wider interests of the nation and, for that reason, I cannot commit myself yet.'

Sir Wally stood up, and lost his temper. (In the reverse order, I think.) 'Come off it, Hacker,' he exploded, 'this is the wrong decision and you know it. It is weak, craven and cowardly.'

Then I got angry. I stood up too. 'I am not a coward.'

'Sit down!' he whispered murderously. His eyes were flashing, and he looked quite ready for a physical punch-up. I decided that discretion was the better part of valour and sat down.

He was beside himself with rage. He was spitting all over my desk as he spoke. 'You think you'll lose a miserable few hundred votes from a few foolish ill-informed people in those constituencies? It's pathetic!'

'It's politics,' I explained.

'Exactly,' he agreed contemptuously, and walked to the door. Then he turned. 'I shall be telephoning the Secretary of State for Industry. I'm prepared to resign if you block this one.'

He stalked out.

We gazed at each other.

After a few moments Sir Humphrey spoke. 'How did you feel that went, Minister?'

I refused to show my concern. As breezily as I could, I replied, 'We'll just have to get another chairman, that's all.'

Humphrey was incredulous. 'Get another? Get *another*? No one else on earth would take that job. *Nobody* wants to be chairman of a nationalised industry. It's instant ruin. They might as well accept the golden handshake on the day they start. It's only a matter of time.'

I still refused to show any concern. 'We'll find someone,' I said, with a confidence that I did not feel.

'Yes,' agreed Humphrey. 'Some useless nonentity or some American geriatric.'

'Not necessarily,' I replied.

'Oh no?' enquired Sir Humphrey. 'So how do you expect the DOI[1] to find a decent replacement when we've forced his predecessor to resign for taking a sound commercial decision which we blocked for political reasons?'

I could see no point in going through all that again. 'I have no choice,' I said simply.

Sir Humphrey tried flattery. 'Minister,' he wheedled. 'A Minister can do what he likes.'

'No,' I explained. 'It's the people's will. I am their leader. I must follow them. I have no guilty conscience. My hands are clean.'

Sir Humphrey stood up, coldly. 'I should have thought,' he remarked, 'that it was frightfully difficult to keep one's hands clean while climbing the greasy pole.'

Then *he* stalked out.

I really was winning friends and influencing people this morning.

I was left with good old faithful Bernard.

We sat and contemplated the various possibilities that could arise from the morning's débâcle. Clearly we had to avoid Wally making a public fuss. We had to stop him giving interviews on *Panorama* or making press statements accusing me of political interference.

I am really on the horns of a dilemma. If I stop the scheme, *The Times* and *The Daily Telegraph* will say that I'm a contemptible political coward. But if I let it go ahead the *Daily Mirror* and the *Sun* will say I'm murdering unborn babies. I can't win!

The only way out is if the Henderson Report had *any* doubt about the safety of metadioxin. But it hasn't. I've read it very carefully.

On the other hand – I've suddenly realised – no one else has read it. Because it's not quite finished. It's still only a *draft* report.

Tomorrow I'll talk to Bernard about this matter. Perhaps the answer is to meet Professor Henderson while there's still time.

[1] Department of Industry.

April 23rd

This morning, at our daily diary session, I asked Bernard if Professor Henderson is a Cambridge man.

Bernard nodded.

'Which college is he at?' I asked casually.

'King's,' said Bernard. 'Why?'

I brushed it aside. 'Just curious – wondered if it was my old college.'

Mistake! 'Weren't you at LSE?' he asked.

'Oh yes, so I was,' I found myself saying. Feeble! I really must do better than that!

I asked Bernard to give me his file, and I asked for a Cambridge telephone directory.

Bernard spoke up bravely. 'Minister . . .' he began nervously '. . . you do realise that . . . not that you have any such intention, of course . . . but, well, it would be most improper to try to influence an independent report of this nature.'

I agreed wholeheartedly that it would be most improper. Unthinkable, in fact. 'But I just thought that we might go and have tea with my old friend R. A. Crichton, Provost of King's.' I told Bernard to get him on the phone.

Bernard did so.

'And,' I added, 'who knows? Professor Henderson might easily drop in for tea with his Provost. That would be a happy coincidence, wouldn't it?'

Bernard thought for a split second, and agreed that it would be perfectly natural, if they were both at the same college.

'There's nothing improper about a coincidence, is there Bernard?'

Deadpan, he replied: 'How can a coincidence be improper, Minister? Impropriety postulates intention, which coincidence precludes.'

Memo: I must learn to use longer words.

April 28th

I had a most satisfactory day up in Cambridge.

Tea with Crichton, my old friend at King's. Now a peer, and very relaxed in academic life.

I asked him how it felt, going from the Commons to the Lords.

'It's like being moved from the animals to the vegetables,' he replied.

By a strange coincidence Professor Henderson had been invited for tea. Crichton introduced us.

Henderson seemed slightly taken aback. 'I must say, I didn't expect to see the Minister,' he said. We both agreed that it was a remarkable coincidence.

Crichton looked astonished and asked if we knew each other. I explained that we'd never met, but that Henderson was writing a report for my Department.

Crichton said that this was quite a coincidence, and Henderson and I both agreed that it was an *amazing* coincidence.

After that we all settled down a bit and, over the Earl Grey, Henderson remarked that I must have been very happy with the draft of his report.

I assured him that I was delighted, absolutely delighted, and I complimented him on his hard work. He, with modesty – and truth – admitted that most of the hard work had been done by the FDA in Washington.

I asked him if he'd ever done a Government report before. He said he hadn't. So I explained that his name will be attached to it forever. THE HENDERSON REPORT.

'A kind of immortality, really,' I added.

He seemed pleased. He smiled, and said he'd never thought of it like that before.

Then I went straight for the jugular. 'But,' I said casually, 'if anything were to go wrong . . .' And I paused.

He was instantly perturbed. 'Go wrong?' His little academic eyes blinked behind his big academic hornrims.

'I mean,' I said gravely, 'if metadioxin is not quite as safe as you say it is. It's your career – this is very courageous of you.'

Professor Henderson was now very concerned. Courageous was manifestly the last thing he ever wanted to be. He was also puzzled, and not quite getting my drift. 'I don't understand,' he said. 'None of the standard tests on metadioxin show any evidence of toxicity.'

I paused for effect. Then: 'None of the *standard* tests. Quite.'

I paused again, while he panicked silently.

'What do you mean?' he said in a high strangled voice that didn't seem to quite belong to this tall fellow with a high forehead and big feet.

I got out my little notebook to refresh my memory. 'Funnily enough,' I explained, 'I was just making a few notes in the train on the way up here. Of course, I'm not a biochemist, you understand, but I'm told that the FDA report leaves some important questions unanswered.'

He thought about this. 'Well . . .' he said finally, and stopped.

I went on: 'And that some of the evidence is inconclusive, that some of the findings have been questioned, and the figures are open to other interpretations.'

Henderson tried to make sense of all this. Then he said: 'But *all* figures are open to . . .'

I interrupted him. 'Absolutely! And that different results might come from a wider and more detailed study over a longer time scale.'

'Well, obviously . . .' he began.

'Yes,' I said firmly. 'You see. If something did go wrong – even in ten years time, a delayed effect – well, the press would go straight to your report. And if it turned out you'd done laboratory trials for a multinational drug company . . .'

He was appalled. 'But that was fifteen years ago.'

'Fourteen,' I corrected him. (This immensely useful piece of information had been revealed by his file). 'And you know what the press are like – "No smoke without fire." Even if there's no real basis. Could be a millstone round your neck.'

I could see that Henderson was wavering, so I piled on the pressure.

'The popular press would be merciless if anything *did* go wrong: DEATH AGONY OF HENDERSON REPORT VICTIMS'.

Henderson was quaking in his shoes. He was in a frightful state. 'Yes, yes, well, I, er, I don't know what to do. I mean. I can't change the evidence. Metadioxin is a safe drug. The report has to say so.'

He looked at me, desperately. I carefully did not fall into the trap. I was not going to make the elementary mistake of telling him what to put in his independent report.

'Quite,' I agreed. 'Quite. I can see you have no choice.'

And I left him.

As I strolled across the room to refill my cup of tea, I saw dear old Crichton slide into my chair and offer Henderson a buttered crumpet.

I knew what he was going to say. He was going to tell Henderson that it's only the phrasing of the Conclusion that you have to worry about. That's the only part the press ever reads.

At the moment it reads: 'On existing evidence, the Committee can see no reason not to proceed.'

I'm sure Crichton will suggest some excellent alternative. And I'm equally sure that Henderson will take his advice.

May 2nd

Victory.

I got the final version of the Henderson Report today. It's all exactly the same, but for the end paragraph, which has undergone the teeniest bit of redrafting.

> While the committee can see no reason not to proceed on the existing evidence, it should be emphasised that Metadioxin is a comparatively recent compound, and it would be irresponsible to deny that after further research its manufacture might be found to be associated with health risks.

I called Bernard at once, and told him to release the report to the press.

Then I cancelled all appointments for today, took a train to Liverpool where another protest meeting was due to take place, the Press Office notified the press, radio and television – and, in a glorious triumphant moment, I announced at the meeting, on television, to an enthusiastic cheering crowd that I would not be giving my approval for the BCC to manufacture Propanol.

I reckon that's four marginals won in the next general election.

When I got home tonight I saw Sir Wally on Newsnight. He made no mention of resignation – he couldn't, of course, he'd been completely out-manoeuvred.

He simply issued a statement in which he said that if the Henderson Report was correct to cast doubt on the safety of metadioxin it was obviously impossible to consider manufacturing it on Merseyside.

May 3rd

Sir Humphrey was angrier with me today than I've ever seen him.

'Do you feel like a hero?' he asked.

'Yes,' I replied. 'Number Ten will be delighted.'

'Probably one of the worst governmental decisions I have ever witnessed,' he snarled. I wasn't bothered by this open rudeness.

'Probably one of the best political decisions I've ever made,' I replied confidently.

Bernard was silent.

110

'What do *you* think, Bernard?' I asked cruelly.

Bernard looked desperate. 'I think . . . that, bearing everything in mind . . . and, ah . . . after due consideration and, well . . . um . . . considering all the implications and, ah, points of view, um, that, well, in other words, I am in fact, *bound* to say that . . . you looked awfully good on television, Minister.'

Having enjoyed watching Bernard wriggle, I turned back to Humphrey. 'Oh by the way,' I asked, 'can we manage a CBE for Henderson? Or a Vice-Chancellorship or something?'

Humphrey was appalled. 'Certainly not! He's completely unreliable and totally lacking in judgement. I still can't think why he suddenly cast doubt on his whole report in that final paragraph.'

'Because,' I replied without thinking, 'he has excellent judgement, enormous stature and great charm.' Then I realised what I'd said.

So did Humphrey. 'I thought you said you'd never met him.' Quick as a flash I replied, 'Intellectual stature.'

Humphrey was not fooled. 'And charm?' he enquired scathingly.

I was almost stumped. 'He . . . er . . . he writes with charm,' I explained unconvincingly. 'Doesn't he Bernard?'

'Yes Minister,' replied Bernard dutifully.

Sir Humphrey's face was a picture.

5

The Devil
You Know

May 4th

The EEC is really intolerably difficult to deal with. For months I have been working with the DAA to get the whole of the Civil Service to place one big central order for word-processing machines. This would replace the present nonsensical practice of every separate department in Whitehall ordering all different sorts of word-processors in dribs and drabs.

If we at the DAA placed one big central order for everyone, the sum of money would be so large it would enable UK manufacturers to make the right sort of investment in systems development.

For days now, we have been on the verge of success. Months of patient negotiations were about to pay off. I was all ready to make a major press announcement: I could see the headlines: HACKER'S MASSIVE INVESTMENT IN MODERN TECHNOLOGY. JIM'S VOTE OF CONFIDENCE IN BRITISH INDUSTRY. BRITAIN CAN MAKE IT, SAYS JIM.

And then, this morning, we got another bloody directive from the bloody EEC in bloody Brussels, saying that all EEC members *must* work to some niggling European word processing standards. And therefore, we must postpone everything in order to agree plans with a whole mass of European Word Processing Committees at the forthcoming European Word Processing Convention in Brussels.

I called a meeting to discuss all this. I went through the whole story so far, and Sir Humphrey and Bernard just sat there saying, 'Yes Minister,' and 'Quite so Minister,' at regular intervals. Some help.

Finally, I got tired of the sound of my own voice. [*Was this a first? – Ed.*] I demanded that Humphrey contribute something to the discussion.

He sighed. 'Well Minister, I'm afraid that this is the penalty we have to pay for trying to pretend that we are Europeans. Believe

112

me, I fully understand your hostility to Europe.'

As so often happens, Humphrey completely missed the point. I tried to explain again.

'Humphrey,' I said slowly and patiently, 'I'm not like you. I am pro-Europe. I'm just anti-Brussels. You seem to be anti-Europe and pro-Brussels.'

He dodged the issue, and pretended that he had no opinions on the EEC. Duplicitous creep. 'Minister, I am neither pro nor anti anything. I am merely a Humble Vessel into which Ministers pour the fruits of their deliberations. But it can certainly be argued that, given the absurdity of the whole European idea, Brussels is in fact doing its best to defend the indefensible and make the unworkable work.'

I told Humphrey that he was talking through his hat and that although I didn't want to sound pompous the European ideal is our best hope of overcoming narrow national self interest.

He told me that I didn't sound pompous – merely inaccurate.

So I explained yet again to the Humble Vessel that Europe is a community of nations united by a common goal.

He chuckled, and I asked if Bernard and I might share the joke.

He was laughing at the idea that the community was united. 'Look at it *objectively*,' he said. 'The game is played for national interests, and always was.'

I disagreed. I reminded him that we went into the EEC to strengthen the international brotherhood of free nations.

Humphrey chukled again. It really was most disconcerting. Then he began to tell me his interpretation – which was even more disconcerting.

'We went in,' he said, 'to screw the French by splitting them off from the Germans. The French went in to protect their inefficient farmers from commercial competition. The Germans went in to cleanse themselves of genocide and apply for readmission to the human race.'

I told Humphrey that I was quite shocked by his appalling cynicism. I couldn't actually argue with what he said because I feel, somewhat uneasily, that there is a ring of truth about it. I said: 'At least the little nations are in it for selfless reasons.'

'Ah yes,' he replied. 'Luxembourg is in it for the perks – all that foreign money pouring into the capital of the EEC.'

'Nonetheless, it's a very sensible location for the capital,' I argued.

He smiled. 'With the administration in Brussels and the Parliament in Strasbourg?' It's like having London as the capital with the House of Commons in Swindon and the Civil Service in Kettering.'

'If this were true,' I said doggedly, 'the other countries wouldn't have been trying to join.'

'Such as?'

'Well, take the Greeks.'

Sir Humphrey settled back reflectively in his chair. 'Actually,' he mused, 'I find it difficult to take the Greeks. Open-minded as I am about foreigners, as well you know.' (His total lack of self-awareness took my breath away!) 'But what will the Greeks want out of it? – an olive mountain and a retsina lake.' He looked at my face, and added apologetically: 'Sorry, I suppose some of your best friends are Greek.'

I could stand no more of this cynical rubbish. I tried to broaden the discussion, to look at the real problems of the community.

'The trouble with Brussels,' I began, 'is not internationalism. It's too much bureaucracy.'

I got no further. Humphrey interrupted me again.

'But don't you see,' he insisted, 'that the bureaucracy is a consequence of the internationalism? Why else would an English Commissioner have a French Director-General immediately below him, an Italian Chef-du-Division reporting to the Frenchman, and so on down the line?'

I was forced to agree. 'I agree,' I said.

'It's the Tower of Babel,' he said.

I was forced to agree again.

'I agree,' I said.

'In fact, it's even worse than that – it's like the United Nations,' he added.

I could not but agree for the third time. 'I agree,' I said.

We both stopped talking and gazed at each other. Where had we reached? What had we decided? What next?

Bernard tried to help out. 'Then, perhaps, if I may interject, perhaps you are in fact in agreement.'

'No we're not!' we said, in unison.

That much was certain!

'Brussels is a shambles,' I said, pursuing my theme of how the bureaucracy destroys the bonds between nations. I reminded Humphrey that the typical Common Market official is said to have the organising capacity of the Italians, the flexibility of the Germans and the modesty of the French. He tops all that up with the imagination of the Belgians, the generosity of the Dutch, and the intelligence of the Irish. Finally for good measure, he has the European spirit of Mr Anthony Wedgwood Benn.[1]

'And now,' I concluded, 'they are all trying to screw up our excellent word-processing plan which is wholly in Britain's interest and my interest.'

'Which are, of course,' added Humphrey, 'one and the same thing.'

I stared at him, and enquired if he was being sarcastic. He denied it. I accepted his denial (though doubtfully) and continued to explore my theory of what's wrong with Brussels.

'The reason that Brussels bureaucrats are so hopeless is not *just* because of the difficulty of running an international organisation – it's because it's a gravy train.'

'A what?' asked Bernard.

'A gravy train,' I repeated, warming to my theme. 'They all live off claret and caviar. Crates of booze in every office. Air-conditioned Mercedes and private planes. Every one of those bureaucrats has got his snout in the trough and most of them have got their front trotters in as well.'

Humphrey, as always, sprang to the defence of the bureaucrats. 'I beg to differ, Minister,' he said reproachfully. 'Brussels is full of hardworking public servants who have to endure a lot of exhausting travel and tedious entertainment.'

Terribly tedious, I thought to myself, working through all that smoked salmon and forcing down all that champagne.

'And in any case Minister,' continued Humphrey, 'you're blaming the wrong people.'

What was he talking about? I'd lost track.

'I understand,' he went on, 'that it was one of your Cabinet colleagues who gave Brussels early warning of your plan for the bulk-buying of word-processors, which is why they have brought this directive out so quickly.'

No wonder I'd lost track. He'd gone back to the point of our conversation. He really is a confusing man to talk to.

And that was it, was it? Betrayed again! By a Cabinet colleague!

[1] A left-wing politician prominent in the 1970s and the early 1980s, a peer's son educated at Westminster and Oxford, chiefly remembered for his lisp, his staring eyes, and his earnest attempts to disguise his privileged background by drinking mugs of tea in worker's co-operatives.

[*Who else? – Ed.*] No prizes for guessing who it was – Basil Corbett! Bloody Basil Corbett! When I think about Basil Corbett I really warm to Judas Iscariot. [*Basil Corbett was another tall, patrician, lisping politician with staring eyes, usually seen smoking a pipe so that people would feel he was 'sound' – Ed.*]

'Corbett?' I asked, though I knew.

Humphrey inclined his head slightly, to indicate that it was indeed the Secretary of State for Trade and Industry who had put the boot in.

I couldn't contain my anger. 'He's a treacherous disloyal, arrogant, opinionated, publicity-seeking creep.' Humphrey gazed at me and said nothing. I mistook his attitude. 'I'm sorry if that sounds harsh, Humphrey,' I added.

'On the contrary, Minister,' replied Humphrey, 'compared with what his Permanent Secretary says, that ranks as a generous tribute.'

I wonder why Corbett did this to me – ah well, time will tell, no doubt.

May 5th

I didn't have to wait long for the answer. Today's *Standard* contained significant and potentially worrying news.

CABINET RESHUFFLE

By Our Political Staff

IT IS being rumoured that the Prime Minister will announce important cabinet changes before the end of the present session. Basil Corbett is rumoured to be

Basil Corbett again. Every time that man comes anywhere near me I get a sharp stabbing pain in the back.

And how come I didn't know about this impending reshuffle? How did they know? I asked Humphrey if it was true.

He was evasive, of course. 'Minister, I am only a humble civil servant. I do not move in such exalted circles as Cabinet Ministers and journalists.'

I persisted. 'Is this rumour true?'

'Yes.'

A straight answer! I was somewhat taken aback. 'How do you know,' I asked, 'if you don't move in such exalted circles?'

'I mean,' he explained, 'it is true that it is rumoured.'

I was worried and anxious. I still am. A reshuffle. This is full of all sorts of implications. I have hardly started on all the things that I planned to do when I got the DAA.

I started to explain this to Humphrey, who pointed out that I may not be moved in a reshuffle. I think he meant to be reassuring, but perhaps he was trying to tell me that my career is not moving forward – which it ought to be.

I asked him if that's what he meant. Again he was evasive. 'At least it wouldn't be moving backwards,' he said.

Backwards? I'd never even considered moving *backwards*! Perhaps he wasn't being evasive after all.

'Look,' I ventured cautiously. 'Tell me. I mean, I'm doing all right, aren't I?'

'Yes indeed, Minister,' he replied smoothly. 'You're doing all right.'

I couldn't quarrel with his words – well, my words, really! – but there seemed to be an air of doubt in his delivery of them.

So I turned to Bernard and said, more positively: 'We're doing all right, aren't we Bernard?'

'Yes Minister.'

That was all. No other words of encouragement seemed to be forthcoming.

I felt I had to justify myself. God knows why! 'Yes' I said. 'Yes. I mean, perhaps I'm not the *outstanding* success of the government, but I'm not a failure, am I?'

'No Minister,' said Bernard, a shade dutifully, I thought. I waited. I was damned if I was going to ask for any compliments. Eventually Bernard said, 'Um – you're doing . . . all right.'

But did he mean it?

And if so, *what* did he mean?

I seemed to be in the throes of an attack of verbal diarrhoea. 'After all,' I said, 'in some ways I've been rather successful. And if Martin goes to the Treasury there's an outside chance I might get the Foreign Office.'

I paused. Nobody spoke. After an eternity Humphrey said, with unmistakable doubt this time, 'Perhaps you might.'

'You don't sound very certain,' I accused him.

To his credit he stuck up for himself. 'I'm not certain, Minister,' he replied, looking me straight in the eye.

I panicked. 'Why not? What have you heard?'

He remained as unperturbed as ever. 'Nothing, Minister, I assure you. That's why I'm not certain.'

I picked up the offending newspaper, stared at it again, and cast it down to the floor.

'Well,' I asked bitterly, 'how does Bob Carver in the *Standard* know all about this reshuffle, if we don't?'

'Perhaps,' speculated Humphrey, 'he has the PM's ear.'

That's the obvious answer – I was forced to agree. 'Yes,' I said. 'Everyone knows that he's in the PM's pocket.'

Bernard perked up. 'Then the PM must have a rather large ear,' he said.

I gave him another withering glance.

I decided not to worry about it any further. I will say no more about it.

It's pointless to worry about it. There's nothing to worry about, anyway.

Yet.

So I briefly discussed the Word Processing Conference in Brussels. Humphrey wants us to go. But it *might* be before the reshuffle.

I asked Humphrey if he knew when the reshuffle would be. After all, it considerably affects the plans I might want to make.

Humphrey's reply was as little help as usual. Something like: 'I'm not privy to the Prime Minister's plans for the projected reshuffle, if indeed there is to be a reshuffle, and I am therefore unaware of any projected date, if indeed there is such a date, and so I think you must proceed on the assumption that the reshuffle will not have happened and make plans for you or your successor accordingly, if indeed you are to have a successor, which of course you may not.'

I decided to decline the invitation. Just in case. I've seen this happen before. This is no time to go on an idiotic foreign junket. One day you're out of your office, the next day you're out of office.

SIR BERNARD WOOLLEY RECALLS:[1]
I well remember that rather tense discussion. Hacker told us no less than six or seven times that he would not worry about the reshuffle, that it was pointless to worry about it and the matter was closed.

[1] In conversation with the Editors.

Then he bit his fingernails a lot.

As he left the office on the way to the Commons, I advised him not to let the reshuffle prey on his mind.

He was most indignant. 'It's not preying on my mind,' he said. 'I've stopped thinking about it.'

And as he left he stopped, turned to me and said: 'Bernard, I'll see you at six o'clock in the House of Shuffles – er, Cards – er, Commons.'

[*During the following week a meeting took place at the Athenaeum Club between Sir Humphrey Appleby, Sir Arnold Robinson (the Cabinet Secretary) and – joining them later – Bernard Woolley. Sir Humphrey wrote a memo, which we found in the DAA Personnel Files at Walthamstow – Ed.*]

Had a meeting with Arnold, who claimed he was unable to give me any details about the impending reshuffle. He said he was merely Cabinet Secretary, not the Political Editor of the *New Standard*.

However, he revealed that Brussels have asked if Hacker would be available for the next Commissionership. It seems it's his if he wants it. A good European and all that.

B.W. [*Bernard Woolley – Ed.*] joined us for coffee. Arnold asked how he felt about having a new Minister. To my astonishment, B.W. said he would be sorry.

Of course, Private Secretaries often feel a certain loyalty to their Ministers, but these feelings must be kept strictly under control. Admitting these sentiments to Sir Arnold is not good for B.W.'s career.

Then, compounding his error, he said that we would all miss Hacker because he was beginning to get a grip on the job.

I sent him home at once.

Subsequently I explained, in confidence, the following essential points on the subject of reshuffles. I told him to commit them to memory.

1) Ministers with a grip on the job are a nuisance because:
  (a) they argue
  (b) they start to learn the facts
  (c) they ask if you have carried out instructions they gave you six months ago
  (d) if you tell them something is impossible, they may dig out an old submission in which you said it was easy
2) When Ministers have gone, we can wipe the slate clean and start again with a new boy
3) Prime Ministers like reshuffles – keeps everyone on the hop
4) Ministers are the *only* people who are frightened of them

B.W. suggested that it would be interesting if Ministers were fixed and Permanent Secretaries were shuffled around. I think he only does it to annoy. He must realise that such a plan strikes at the very heart of the system that has made Britain what she is today.

Just to be safe I instructed B.W. to memorise the following three points:

119

> Power goes with permanence
> Impermanence is impotence
> And rotation is castration

Talking of which, I think that perhaps Bernard should be given a new posting before too long.

[The following day, Sir Humphrey received a crucial piece of information in a note from Sir Arnold – Ed.]

1O DOWNING STREET

From the Cabinet Secretary

May 9th

Dear Humpy,

Don't get out the champagne too soon. If Hacker takes Brussels, I'm sorry to say that you may get B.C.[1]

Yours ever,

A.

[Hacker was naturally in complete ignorance of the above information. His diaries continue overleaf – Ed.]

[1] Basil Corbett.

May 11th

Still no news of the reshuffle.

I've been sitting up till late, doing my boxes. Three of them, tonight.

The papers were still full of rumours about the reshuffle. Annie asked me tonight if they're true.

I told her I didn't know.

She was surprised. She thought I was bound to know, as I'm in the Cabinet. But that's the whole point – we'll be the last to know.

Annie suggested I ask the PM. But obviously I can't – it would make me look as though I were insecure.

The trouble is, I don't know whether it'll be good news. I explained this to Annie. 'I don't know whether I'll be going up or down.'

'Or just round and round, as usual,' she said.

I asked her if, quite seriously, she thought I'd been a success. Or a failure.

She said: 'I think you've done all right.'

'But is that good enough?'

'I don't know,' she said. 'Is it?'

'I don't know,' I replied. 'Is it?'

We sat and looked at each other. It's so hard to tell. I had a sudden thought.

'Perhaps the PM might think I'm becoming too successful. A possible challenge to the leadership.'

Annie looked up from her book, and blinked. 'You?' she asked.

I hadn't actually meant me, as such, though I wasn't all that pleased that she was *so* surprised.

'No,' I explained, 'Martin. But with my support. So if the PM is trying to repel boarders and if Martin can't be got rid of safely, which he can't, not the Foreign Secretary, then . . . I'm the obvious one to be demoted. Do you see? Isolate Martin.'

She asked where I could be sent. 'That's easy. Lord President, Lord Privy Seal, Minister for the Arts, Minister for Sport in charge of Floods and Droughts – there's no shortage of useless non-jobs. And Basil Corbett is out to get me,' I reminded Annie.

'He's out to get everyone,' she pointed out. That's true.

'He's a smooth-tongued, cold-eyed, hard-nosed, two-faced creep,' I said, trying to be fair.

She was puzzled. 'How is he so successful?'

'Because,' I explained, 'he's a smooth-tongued, cold-eyed, hard-nosed, two-faced creep.'

Also he's got a good television manner, a lot of grassroots party support (though *all* the MPs hate him), and he has somehow conned the public into believing he's sincere.

His biggest and best weapon is elbows. I've got to elbow Corbett out of the way, or else he'll elbow me. I explained to Annie that elbows are the most important weapon in a politician's armory.

'Other than integrity,' she said.

I'm afraid I laughed till I cried. Tears rolled down my face. It took me five minutes to get my breath back – what made it even funnier was Annie staring at me, uncomprehending, as if I'd gone mad.

I didn't really get my breath back till the phone rang. To my enormous surprise it was Gaston Larousse – from Brussels.

'Good evening Commissionaire,' I said. Perhaps I should have just said Commissioner.

He was calling me to enquire if I'd let my name go forward as a commissioner of the EEC. I told him I was honoured, that I'd have to think about it, thanked him for thinking of me, etc. I asked him if Number Ten knew about it. He was evasive, but eventually said yes.

[*Notes of this phone call discovered many years later among Gaston Larrousse's papers suggest that he was not intentionally evasive. Hacker, presumably in an attempt to show that he was a linguist, enquired if* Numero Dix *knew about the offer. Larousse did not initially equate* Numero Dix *with Number Ten Downing Street – Ed.*]

What does this mean?

I discussed it with Annie. Obviously, it would mean living in Brussels, as she pointed out.

But what does it *mean? Really* mean? Is it a plot by Number Ten to ease me out? Or is it a coincidence? Is it a hint? Is the PM giving me a face-saving exit? If so, why hasn't Number Ten told me? Or is it nothing to do with the PM? Was the vacancy coming up anyway? And it's a great honour – isn't it? Why is my life always so full of unanswerable questions?

Annie thought of another question. 'Is it a good job?'

I shook my head. 'It's a terrible job. It would be curtains for me as far as British politics is concerned. Worse than getting a peerage. Complete failure. You're reduced to forming a new party to try and get back.'

Annie asked what the job involved.

I began to list it all. 'Well,' I told her, 'you're right in the heart of that ghastly European bureaucracy. It's one big gravy train: fifty thousand a year salary, twenty thousand pounds expense account. All champagne and lobsters. Banquets. Overseas visits. Luxury hotels. Limousines and chauffeurs and private aircraft and siestas after lunch and weekends on the beach at Knocke-le-Zoutte . . .' I suddenly realised what I was saying. It's strange how you can talk and talk and not hear yourself – not hear the implications of what you're saying.

'Perhaps,' I finished, 'we should go over there and have a look.'

Annie looked hopeful. 'Why not?' she said. 'Sometimes I think we deserve a bit of failure.'

May 12th

Had an interesting conversation with Roy[1] this morning. Of course, he knew all about the reshuffle.

I assumed he'd read it in the *Standard* like me – but no, he first heard of it a couple of weeks ago. (Why didn't he tell *me*? He knows that I rely on him to keep me fully informed.)

But it seems he assumed I knew. *All* the drivers knew. They knew it from the PM's driver and the Cabinet Secretary's driver – apparently it's been an open secret.

Casually, I asked him what *he'd* heard – trying thereby to suggest that I had also heard things. Which I haven't, of course.

'Just the usual, sir,' he replied. 'Corbett's in line for promotion, the PM can't overlook him. And apparently old Fred – sorry guv, I mean the Employment Secretary – he's going to get the push. Kicked upstairs.'

He seemed utterly confident about this. I asked him how he knew.

'His driver's been reassigned.'

'And what's the gossip about me?'

'Nothing, sir.'

Nothing! Was he telling the truth? There must be *some* gossip about me. I'm in the bloody Cabinet, for God's sake.

'Funny, isn't it?' said Roy. 'My mates and I haven't known what to make of that.' He gave me a sly look in the rear view mirror. ''Course, you'll know what's happening to you, won't you sir?'

He knew bloody well I've not the faintest idea. I think. Or else he was trying to find out. More information to barter in the transport pool.

'Yes, of course,' I replied, vaguely. I should have left it at that,

[1] Hacker's driver.

but it was like picking at a scab. ''Course, it's hard to tell about one-self sometimes – you know, whether one's a success, or . . .' He didn't come to the rescue. I tried again. 'Do your mates, er . . .'

He interrupted me, somewhat patronisingly.

'They all think you've done all right, sir.'

Again!

May 13th

Yesterday was full of meetings. Cabinet, Cabinet Committee, three-line whip in the house – I got very little time with Bernard. Not enough for a real conversation.

But Bernard's always given me loyal support, he's a bright fellow, and I decided to seek his advice.

I told him, over a cup of tea this afternoon, that I'm in a bit of a quandary.

'There's this reshuffle on the cards,' I began.

He chuckled. I couldn't see why. Then he apologised. 'I'm so sorry, Minister, I thought you were making a . . . do go on.'

'To complicate matters, and I tell you this in complete confidence, I've been approached about becoming one of Britain's EEC Commissioners in Brussels.'

'How very nice,' said Bernard.

'But *is* it nice?' I seized upon his reply. 'That's my dilemma.' He said nothing. I asked him if he really thought that, as Minister at the DAA, I'd done all right.

I suppose I was hoping for high praise. 'Superbly' would have been a nice answer. As it was, Bernard nodded and said, 'Yes, you've done all right.'

It seems that no one is prepared to commit themselves further than that on the subject of my performance. It really is rather dis-couraging. And it's not my fault I've not been a glittering success, Humphrey has blocked me on so many issues, he's never really been on my side. 'Look, let's be honest,' I said to Bernard. '*All right* isn't good enough, is it?'

'Well . . . it's all right,' he replied carefully.

So I asked him if he'd heard any rumours on the grapevine. About me.

He replied, 'Nothing, really.' And then, incredibly: 'Only that the British Commissioner in Europe sent a telegram to the FCO [*Foreign and Commonwealth Office – Ed.*] and to the Cabinet Committee on Europe, that the idea for you to be a Commissioner came from

Brussels but that it is – at the end of the day – a Prime Ministerial appointment. The Prime Minister has in fact discussed it extensively with the Secretary of State for Foreign Affairs and the Secretary to the Cabinet, and cleared the way for you to be sounded out on the subject. As it is believed at Number Ten that you might well accept such an honour, a colleague of yours has been sounded out about becoming our Minister here at the DAA.' He paused, then added apologetically, 'I'm afraid that's all I know.'

'No more than that?' I asked with heavy irony.

I then asked which colleague had been sounded out to replace me at the DAA. Bernard didn't know.

But I was really getting nowhere with my basic problem. Which is, if I don't go to Europe will I be pushed up, or down – or out!

May 14th
Rumours suggest that the reshuffle is imminent. The papers are full of it. Still no mention of me, which means the lobby correspondents have been told nothing one way or the other.

It's all very nerve-racking. I'm quite unable to think about any of my ministerial duties. I'm becoming obsessed with my future – or lack of it. And I must decide soon whether to accept or decline Europe.

I had a meeting with Sir Humphrey today. It was supposed to be on the subject of the Word Processing Conference in Brussels.

I opened it up by telling Humphrey that I'd changed my mind. 'I've decided to go to Brussels,' I said. I meant go and have a look, as I'd arranged with Annie. But Humphrey misunderstood me.

'You're not resigning from the Department of Administrative Affairs?' he asked. He seemed shocked. I was rather pleased. Perhaps he has a higher opinion of me than I realised.

I put him out of his misery. 'Certainly not. I'm talking about this Word Processing Conference.'

He visibly relaxed. Then I added, 'But I would like to see Brussels for myself.'

'Why?' he asked.

'Why not?' I asked him.

'Why not indeed?' he asked me. 'But why?' he repeated.

I told him I was curious. He agreed.

Then I told him, preparing the ground for my possible permanent departure across the Channel, that I felt on reflection that I'd been a bit hasty in my criticisms of Brussels and that I'd found Humphrey's defence of it thoroughly convincing.

This didn't please him as much as I'd expected. He told me that he had been reflecting on *my* views, that he had found much truth and wisdom in my criticism of Brussels. (Was this Humphrey speaking? I had to pinch myself to make sure I wasn't dreaming.)

'You implied it was corrupt, and indeed you have opened my eyes,' he said.

'No, no, no,' I said hastily.

'Yes, yes,' he replied firmly.

I couldn't allow Humphrey to think that I'd said it was corrupt. I *had* said it, actually, but now I'm not so sure. [*We are not sure whether Hacker was not sure that he wanted to be quoted or not sure that Brussels was corrupt – Ed.*] I told Humphrey that he had persuaded *me*. I can now see, quite clearly, that Brussels is full of dedicated men carrying a heavy burden of travel and entertainment – they need all that luxury and the odd drinkie.

'Champagne and caviar?' enquired Sir Humphrey. 'Private planes, air-conditioned Mercedes?'

I reminded Humphrey that these little luxuries oil the diplomatic wheels.

'Snouts in the trough,' remarked Humphrey, to no one in particular.

I reproved him. 'That is not an attractive phrase,' I said coldly.

'I'm so sorry', he said. 'I can't think where I picked it up.'

I drew the discussion to a close by stating that we would all go to Brussels next week to attend this conference, as he had originally requested.

As he got up to leave, Humphrey asked me if my change of heart about Brussels was entirely the result of his arguments.

Naturally, I told him yes.

He didn't believe me. 'It wouldn't be anything to do with rumours of your being offered a post in Brussels?'

I couldn't let him know that he was right. 'The thought is not worthy of you, Humphrey,' I said. And, thinking of Annie and trying not to laugh, I added solemnly: 'There is such a thing as integrity.'

Humphrey looked confused.

[*Later that day Sir Humphrey had lunch with Sir Arnold Robinson, Secretary to the Cabinet, at their club. He made the following note in his private diary – Ed.*]

I told Arnold that I was most concerned about letting Corbett loose on the DAA. I would regard it as a disaster of the utmost magnitude.

Arnold said that he was unable to stop the move. The Prime Minister appoints the Cabinet. I refused to accept this explanation – we all know perfectly well that the Cabinet Secretary arranges reshuffles. I said as much.

Arnold acknowledged this fact but insisted that, if the PM is really set on making a particular appointment, the Cabinet Secretary must reluctantly acquiesce.

I remain convinced that Arnold keeps a hand on the tiller.

[*The matter rested there until Sir Humphrey Appleby received a memo from Sir Arnold Robinson, see overleaf – Ed.*]

A memo from Sir Arnold Robinson to Sir Humphrey Appleby:

1O DOWNING STREET

From the Secretary to the Cabinet

May 16ᵗʰ

Dear Humpy,

Have been considering your problem
further. I think the only answer to your
problem is for J.H. to turn Brussels down.

A.

A reply from Sir Humphrey Appleby:

MINISTRY OF
ADMINISTRATIVE AFFAIRS

From the Permanent Under Secretary of State

Dear Arnold,

I think he's going to take Brussels. He says he believes in the European ideal! Extraordinary, isn't it? I fear he's been taken in by his own speeches.

Also, I fear he regards himself as not having been a total success at the D.A.A.

HA

16/v

A reply from Sir Arnold:

1O DOWNING STREET

From the Secretary of State to the Cabinet   May 17th

Dear Humpy,

    He's not been all that hot. Partly your fault. You've blocked him continually, albeit in the interests of good government.

    I suggest that Hacker has a big success within the next couple of days.

A.

A reply from Sir Humphrey:

MINISTRY OF
ADMINISTRATIVE AFFAIRS

From the Permanent Under Secretary of State

Arnold —

A big success? In the next two days?
What sort of success?

JA

17/v

A reply from Sir Arnold:

10 DOWNING STREET

From the Secretary of State to the Cabinet   May 18th

Humpy,

Anything, my dear chap. Just give me some sort of case to present to the P.M. for keeping Hacker at the D.A.A.

There is one other possibility for Corbett: Dept of Employment. Fred is definitely going, because he keeps falling asleep in Cabinet — I know they all do, but Fred has taken to nodding off while he's actually talking.

A.

May 21st

I was still paralysed with indecision as today began.

At my morning meeting with Humphrey I asked if he had any news. He denied it. I know he had lunch with the Cabinet Secretary a couple of days ago – is it conceivable that Arnold Robinson told him nothing?

'You must know something?' I said firmly.

Slight pause.

'All I know, Minister, is that the reshuffle will definitely be announced on Monday. Have *you* any news?'

I couldn't think what he meant.

'Of Brussels,' he added. 'Are you accepting the Commissionership?'

I tried to explain my ambivalence. 'Speaking with my Parliamentary hat on, I think it would be a bad idea. On the other hand, with my Cabinet hat on, I can see that it might be quite a good idea. But there again, with my European hat on, I can see that there are arguments on both sides.'

I couldn't believe the rubbish I could hear myself talking. Humphrey and Bernard might well have wondered which hat I was talking through at the moment.

They simply gazed at me, silent and baffled.

Humphrey then sought elucidation.

'Minister, does that mean you have decided you want to go to Brussels?'

'Well . . .' I replied, 'yes and no.'

I found that I was enjoying myself for the first time for days.

Humphrey tried to help me clarify my mind.

He asked me to list the pros and cons.

This threw me into instant confusion again. I told him I didn't really know what I think, thought, because – and I don't know if I'd mentioned this to Humphrey before, I think I *might* have – it all rather depends on whether or not I've done all right. So I asked Humphrey how he thought I'd done.

Humphrey said he thought I'd done all right.

So I was no further on. I'm going round and round in circles. If I've done all right, I mean *really* all right, then I'll stay because I'll be all right. But if I've only done all right, I mean only *just* all right, then I think to stay here wouldn't be right – it would be wrong, right?

Humphrey then appeared to make a positive suggestion. 'Minister,' he volunteered, 'I think that, to be on the safe side, you need a big personal success.'

Great, I thought! Yes indeed.

'A triumph, in fact,' said Humphrey.

'Like what?'

'I mean,' said Humphrey, 'some great personal publicity for a great personal and political achievement.'

I was getting rather excited. I waited expectantly. But suddenly Humphrey fell silent.

'Well . . .' I asked, 'what have you in mind?'

'Nothing,' he said. 'I'm trying to think of something.'

That was a great help!

I asked what the purpose would be of this hypothetical triumph. He told me that Sir Arnold indicated that the PM would be unable to move me downwards if I had a triumph before the reshuffle.

That's obvious. What's even more worrying is the implication that there was no possibility of the PM moving me upwards.

I mentioned this. Humphrey replied that, alas! one must be a realist. I don't think he realised just how insulting he was being.

I told Humphrey I'd take Brussels, and brought the meeting to a close. I decided I'd call Brussels tonight and accept the post, and thus avoid the humiliation of being demoted in the Cabinet by pre-empting the PM.

I told Humphrey he could go, and instructed Bernard to bring me details of the European Word-Processing standardisation plans, to which I would now be fully committed.

Then Humphrey had an idea.

He stood up, excitedly.

'Wait a minute,' he said, 'I have an idea. Supposing you were to ignore the EEC and publish your *own* plan for word processing equipment, and place huge contracts with British manufacturers, immediately, today, tomorrow, well *before Monday*, thus ensuring more jobs in Britain, more investment, more export orders . . .'

He looked at me.

I tried to readjust my thoughts. Weren't we back at square one? This is what I'd been about to do before we got the directive from Brussels a couple of weeks ago. And Humphrey had told me that we had to comply with a Brussels directive.

'It's not a directive,' he now explained. 'It hasn't been ratified by the Convention. It's a request.'

I wondered, aloud, if we could really stab our partners in the back, and spit in their faces.

Bernard intervened. 'You can't stab anyone in the back while you spit in their face,' I suppose he was trying to be helpful.

The more I thought about it, the more I realised that Humphrey's scheme had a touch of real genius about it. Defying Brussels would be very popular in the country. It would be a big story. And it would prove that I had elbows.

I told Humphrey that it was a good idea.

'You'll do it?' he asked.

I didn't want to be rushed. 'Let me think about it,' I said. 'After all, it would mean giving up . . .' I didn't know how to put it.

'The trough?' he offered.

'No, that's *not* what I meant,' I replied coldly, though actually it was what I meant.

He knew it was anyway, because he said: 'When it comes to it, Minister, one must put one's country first.'

On the whole, I suppose I agree with that.

May 23rd

JIM FIXES THEM!
Big boost for Britain!

ADMINISTRATIVE AFFAIRS supremo Jim Hacker today gave the Common Market one in the eye. In a move that will be very popular throughout the country, he told our European partners that Britain would go it alone in information technology.

My repudiation of the EEC request had indeed proved to be a big story. A triumph, in fact. Especially as I accompanied it with a rather jingoistic anti-Brussels speech. The popular press loved it, but I'm afraid that I've irrevocably burned my boats – I don't think I'll be offered a Commissionership again in a hurry.

Let's hope it does the trick.

May 24th

The reshuffle was announced today. Fred was indeed kicked upstairs, Basil Corbett went to Employment, and I stayed where I am – at the DAA.

Humphrey popped in first thing, and told me how delighted he was that I was staying.

'I know I probably shouldn't say this, but I personally would have been deeply sorry to lose you.' He told me that he meant it most sincerely.

'Yes,' I said benignly, 'we've grown quite fond of each other really, haven't we, like terrorist and a hostage.'

He nodded.

'Which of you is the terrorist?' asked Bernard.

'He is,' Humphrey and I said it in unison, each pointing at the other.

Then we all laughed.

'By the way,' I asked, 'who would have had my job if I'd gone to Brussels?'

'I've no idea,' said Humphrey.

But Bernard said: 'Didn't you tell me it was to be Basil Corbett, Sir Humphrey?'

A bucket of cold water had been thrown over our temporary spirit of bonhomie. Humphrey looked more embarrassed than I've ever seen him. No wonder he would have been so sorry to lose me.

I looked at him for confirmation.

'Basil Corbett?' I asked.

'Yes Minister,' said Sir Humphrey. And he blushed.

6

The Quality
of Life

[*Early in May Sir Humphrey Appleby started negotiations with the Merchant Bank of which Sir Desmond Glazebrook was the Chairman. Sir Desmond had been appointed Chairman of the Co-Partnership Commission the previous year by Hacker, at Appleby's instigation, in order to get them both off the hook of the Solihull Report scandal. See Volume One.*

In May of this year Sir Humphrey was negotiating for a seat on the Board of the Bank when he retired three or four years hence. Sir Humphrey Appleby still had not received his G, nor had he sewn up a suitable retirement position for himself. Recent encounters with Sir Arnold Robinson (see Chapter 2) suggested that, although it was not impossible that he would become the next Secretary to the Cabinet, he was probably not the front-runner. He was known to be anti-Europe, so a Director-Generalship in Brussels seemed unlikely to be offered. He was therefore most anxious to ensure the seat on the board of Sir Desmond's bank – Ed.]

May 25th

Excellent coverage in the press today for my speech on the environment last night.

Headlines in a couple of the quality dailies: HACKER SPEAKS OUT AGAINST TOWER BLOCKS and MINISTER'S COURAGEOUS STAND ON HIGH BUILDINGS, though the latter does make me sound more like Harold Lloyd than a Minister of the Crown. Still, to be called courageous by a newspaper is praise indeed.

But all this coverage in the posh press, though nice, isn't worth all that much in votes. There was no coverage of my speech in the popular press. It's weeks since I had my photo in any of the mass circulation dailies.

So I called in Bill Pritchard, the press officer, and asked his advice. He thought for a moment or two.

'Well,' he offered, 'the papers always like a photograph of a pretty girl.'

Brilliant. I pointed out that, although it may have escaped his notice, I did not qualify on that score. But he went on to suggest that I judge a bathing beauty contest, kiss the winner, that sort of thing. A cheap stunt really, and rather old hat. Besides, if my picture's going to be in the paper I'd like the readers to look at *me*.

Then he suggested animals and children. He pointed out that tomorrow's visit to a City Farm will almost certainly yield good publicity. Apparently it's to be covered by the *Mirror*, *Mail*, *Express*, *Sun*, and 'Today' and 'Nationwide'.

This is marvellous. Telly coverage is the best of all, of course. And an innocuous non-controversial venue like a City Farm can't possibly contain any hidden pitfalls.

Bill told me that Sue Lawley wanted to interview me. And that I was to be photographed with some baby donkeys at the *Sun*'s special request.

Sometimes I think he's got no sense at all! Even if the *Sun* has no ulterior motive (which I doubt) it would be a gift for *Private Eye* – JAMES HACKER WITH A CROWD OF OTHER DONKEYS or A MEETING OF THE INNER CABINET.

I refused. He offered little pigs instead. I don't think that my being photographed with a crowd of little pigs is any great improvement! That could give rise to SNOUTS IN THE TROUGH jokes.

I told Bill to pull himself together, and that I'd agree to be photographed with Sue Lawley or a nice woolly lamb. Positively no one else.

[*Politicians frequently try to avoid making public appearances that could give rise to jokes at their expense. For instance, when Harold Wilson was PM in the late 1960s some of his advisers suggested that perhaps he shouldn't go to* Fiddler on the Roof *as it might encourage jokes about his leadership style. He also avoided going to visit* A Month in the Country *as it was feared that this would give rise to dangerous speculation that he was going to the country, i.e. calling a general election – Ed.*]

At my diary session later this morning Bernard said that Sir Desmond Glazebrook wanted an urgent meeting with me tomorrow. He's a ridiculous old fool who keeps making speeches against the government. Unfortunately, I appointed him Chairman of the Co-Partnership Commission – I'd had no choice [*see Volume One*,

Chapter 7 Jobs for the Boys – Ed.]

Glazebrook wants to talk to me about his forthcoming application to add some more storeys to his bank's proposed new office block.

Clearly he hasn't read this morning's papers!

This is just the sort of thing we have to stop. Someone has to speak out to save the environment. I shall do it, without fear or favour. It is the right thing to do. Also, it'll be very popular.

[*Bernard Woolley reported this conversation with Hacker to Sir Humphrey Appleby sometime later that day. He knew that Appleby was due to meet Sir Desmond Glazebrook for tea, to discuss the new high-rise building for the bank, and he felt obliged to let Sir Humphrey know the extent of the Minister's opposition to it.*

We found a report of this and of Appleby's meeting with Glazebrook among Sir Humphrey's private papers – Ed.]

B. reported to me that the Minister wanted to make a courageous stand on high buildings, for the press. I hope he has a head for heights. It seems that Hacker will do anything to get his picture in the papers.

Had tea with Sir Desmond, and reported that the matter did not look too hopeful. He was surprised. I remarked that, clearly, he had not read the *Financial Times* this morning.

'Never do,' he told me. I was surprised. He is a banker after all.

'Can't understand it,' he explained. 'Its too full of economic theory.'

I asked him why he bought it and carried it about under his arm. He explained that it was part of the uniform. He said it took him thirty years to understand Keynes's economics and just when he'd finally got the hang of it everyone started getting hooked on those new fangled monetarist ideas. Books like *I want to be free* by Milton Shulman.

Presumably he means *Free To Choose* by Milton Friedman, but I share his feelings and doubts.

He asked me why they are all called Milton, and said he was still stuck on Milton Keynes. I corrected him: 'Maynard Keynes.' He said he was sure there was a Milton Keynes, I felt the conversation should be abandoned then and there, and I opened up his copy of the *FT* and showed him our Minister's speech to the Architectural Association last night in which he attacked skyscraper blocks. This speech has attracted much favourable publicity and must be reckoned a problem for us now.

Sir Desmond insisted that the bank's new block is not a skyscraper. Nonetheless, it has thirty-eight storeys on current plans, and he is asking for an extra six storeys.

The Minister, on the other hand, is talking about a maximum tolerable height of eight storeys.

The Minister is further encouraged by his party's manifesto, which contained a promise to prevent many more high-rise buildings. But this problem is more easily dealt with. I explained to Sir Desmond that there is an implicit pact offered to every Minister by his senior officials: if the Minister will help us implement the opposite policy to the one to which he is pledged (which once he is in office he can see is obviously undesirable and/or unworkable) we will help him to pretend that he is in fact doing what he said he was going to do in his Manifesto.

[*We are indeed fortunate that Sir Humphrey's training as a civil servant – training to put everything down in writing – resulted in his recording for posterity these attitudes and skills which were undoubtedly Civil Service practice in the 1980s but which were kept secret because they were unacceptable constitutionally – Ed.*]

Desmond said that this was a reasonable compromise, in his opinion. So it is. Regrettably, reasonableness is not the first quality that springs to mind when one contemplates the average Minister. [*And Hacker was very average – Ed.*]

Desmond tried to apply pressure to me. He dropped hints about our future plans together. I reassured Desmond that, although he would not get permission from Hacker this week and although it would be tricky, I was sure a way could be found to alter any adverse decision.

Desmond was puzzled. He thought a decision was a decision. I explained that a decision is a decision *only* if it is the decision you wanted. Otherwise, of course, it is merely a temporary setback.

Ministers are like small children. They act on impulse. One day they want something desperately, the next day they've forgotten they ever asked for it. Like a tantrum over a rice pudding – won't touch it today and asks for two helpings tomorrow.

Desmond asked me if I intended to tell him that I refused to accept his decision. The man really is dense! I explained that, on the contrary, I shall start off by accepting Hacker's decision enthusiastically. Then I shall tell him to leave the details to me. [*Appleby Papers 97/JZD/31f*]

[*Hacker's diary continues – Ed.*]

May 26th

We had the urgent meeting with Sir Desmond Glazebrook today. It went off most satisfactorily and presented no problems, largely because it was preceded by a meeting between me and Sir Humphrey in which I ensured his full co-operation and support.

When Humphrey popped in for a quick word before the meeting he outlined Glazebrook's case for a tower block:

1) There are already several tower blocks in the area

2) Their International Division is expanding rapidly and needs space. And international work brings in valuable invisible exports

3) Banks need central locations. They can't move some of it elsewhere

4) It will bring in extra rate revenue for the city

This is a not unreasonable case. But, as I pointed out to Humphrey, it's a typical bank argument, money, money, money! What about the environment? What about the beauty?

Humphrey was impressed. 'Indeed Minister,' he agreed. 'Beauty. Quite.' He told Bernard to make a note of it.

I could see I was winning. 'And what about our children? And our children's children?'

Again he agreed, and told Bernard to be sure he make a note of 'children's children'.

'Who are you serving, Humphrey?' I asked. 'God or Mammon?'

'I'm serving you, Minister,' he replied.

Quite right. I told Bernard to show Glazebrook in, and Sir Humphrey said to me: 'Minister, it's entirely your decision. Entirely your decision.' I think he's getting the idea at last! That I'm the boss!

Desmond Glazebrook arrived with an architect named Crawford, complete with plans. They began by explaining that they would be making a formal application later, but they'd be grateful for any guidance that I could give them at this stage.

That was easy. I told them that I had grave misgivings about these tower blocks.

'Dash it, this is where we make our profits,' said Sir Desmond. 'Six extra storeys and we'll really clean up. Without them we'll only make a measly twenty-eight per cent on the whole project.'

I stared at him coldly. 'It's just profits, is it, Sir Desmond?'

He looked confused. 'Not *just* profits,' he said, 'it's profits!'

'Do you ever think of anything except money?' I asked him.

Again he looked completely blank. 'No. Why?'

'You don't think about beauty?'

'Beauty?' He had no idea what I was driving at. 'This is an office block, not an oil painting.'

I persevered. 'What about the environment?' I enquired.

'Well . . .' he said, looking at Humphrey for help. Sir Humphrey, to his credit, gave him none. 'Well, I promise you we'll make sure it's part of the environment. I mean, it's bound to be, once it's there, isn't it?'

I had reached my decision. 'The answer's no,' I said firmly.

Crawford the architect intervened. 'There is just one thing, Minister,' he said timidly. 'As you will remember from the papers, similar permission has already been given for the Chartered Bank of New York, so to refuse it to a British bank. . . .'

I hadn't realised. Bernard or Humphrey should have briefed me more thoroughly.

I didn't answer for a moment, and Sir Desmond chipped in:

'So it's all right after all, is it?'

'No it's not,' I snapped.

'Why not, dammit?' he demanded.

I was stuck. I had to honour our manifesto commitment, and I couldn't go back on my widely-reported speech yesterday. But if we'd given permission to an American bank . . .

Thank God, Humphrey came to the rescue!

'The Minister,' he said smoothly, 'has expressed concern that a further tall building would clutter the skyline.'

I seized on this point gratefully. 'Clutter the skyline,' I repeated, with considerable emphasis.

'He is also worried,' continued Sir Humphrey, 'that more office workers in that area would mean excessive strain on the public transport system.'

He looked at me for support, and I indicated that I was indeed worried about public transport. Humphrey was really being most creative. Very impressive.

'Furthermore,' said Humphrey, by now unstoppable, 'the Minister pointed out that it would overshadow the playground of St James's Primary School here . . .' (he pointed to the map) 'and that it would overlook a number of private gardens, which would be an intrusion of privacy.'

'Privacy,' I agreed enthusiastically.

'Finally,' said Humphrey, lying through his teeth, 'the Minister also pointed out, most astutely if I may say so, that your bank owns a vacant site a short way away, which would accommodate your expansion needs.'

Sir Desmond looked at me. 'Where?' he asked.

I stabbed wildly at the map with my finger. 'Here,' I said.

Desmond looked closely. 'That's the river, isn't it?'

I shook my head with pretended impatience at his stupidity, and again Humphrey saved the day. 'I think the Minister was referring to *this* site,' he said, and pointed with precision.

Sir Desmond looked again.

'Is that ours?' he asked.

'It is, actually, Sir Desmond,' whispered Crawford.

'What are we doing with it?'

'It's scheduled for Phase III.'

Sir Desmond turned to me and said, as if I hadn't heard, 'That's scheduled for Phase III. Anyway,' he went on, 'that's at least four hundred yards away. Difficult for the Board to walk four hundred yards for lunch. And impossible to walk four hundred yards back afterwards.'

I felt that I'd spent enough time on this pointless meeting. I brought it to a close.

'Well, there it is,' I said. 'You can still put in your formal application, but that will be my decision, I'm sure.'

Bernard opened the door for Sir Desmond, who stood up very reluctantly.

'Suppose we design a different rice pudding?' he said.

I think he must be suffering from premature senility.

'Rice pudding?' I asked.

Humphrey stepped in, tactful as ever. 'It's er . . . it's bankers jargon for high rise buildings, Minister.'

'Is it?' asked Sir Desmond.

Poor old fellow.

After he'd gone I thanked Humphrey for all his help. He seemed genuinely pleased.

I made a point of thanking him *especially* because I know that he and Desmond Glazebrook were old chums.

'We've known each other a long time, Minister,' he replied, 'But even a lifelong friendship is as naught compared with a civil servant's duty to support his Minister.'

Quite right too.

Then I had to rush off to my public appearance at the City Farm.

Before I left, Humphrey insisted that I sign some document. He said it was urgent. An administrative order formalising government powers for temporary utilisation of something-or-other. He gave me some gobbledegook explanation of why I had to sign it rather than its being put before the House. Just some piece of red tape.

But I wish he wouldn't always try to explain these things to me when he can see I'm late for some other appointment.

Not that it matters much.

SIR BERNARD WOOLLEY RECALLS:[1]

Hacker was being thoroughly bamboozled by Sir Humphrey and was completely unaware of it.

[1] In conversation with the Editors.

The Administrative Order in question was to formalise government powers for the temporary utilisation of unused local authority land until development commences, when of course it reverts to the authority.

In answer to Hacker's question as to why it was not being laid before the House, Sir Humphrey gave the correct answer. He explained that if it were a statutory instrument it would indeed have to be laid on the table of the House, for forty days, assuming it were a negative order, since an affirmative order would, of course necessitate a vote, but in fact it was not a statutory instrument nor indeed an Order in Council but simply an Administrative order made under Section 7, subsection 3 of the Environmental Administration Act, which was of course an enabling section empowering the Minister to make such regulations affecting small scale land usage as might from time to time appear desirable within the general framework of the Act.

After he had explained all this, to Hacker's evident incomprehension, he added humorously, 'as I'm sure you recollect only too clearly, Minister.' Appleby really was rather a cad!

I must say, though, that even I didn't grasp the full significance of this move that afternoon. I didn't even fully comprehend, in those days, why Humphrey had persuaded Hacker to sign the document on the pretext that it was urgent.

'It was not urgent,' he explained to me later, 'but it was important. Any document that removes the power of decision from Ministers and gives it to us is important.'

I asked why. He rightly ticked me off for obtuseness. Giving powers of decision to the Service helps to take government out of politics. That was, in his view, Britain's only hope of survival.

The urgency was true in one sense, of course, in that whenever you want a Minister to sign something without too many questions it is always better to wait until he is in a hurry. That is when their concentration is weakest. Ministers are always vulnerable when they are in a hurry.

That is why we always kept them on the go, of course.

[Hacker's diary for that day continues – Ed.]
It's always hard to find something to make a speech about. We have to make a great many speeches, of course – local authority elections, bye-elections, GLC elections, opening village fêtes or the new old people's home, every weekend in my constituency there's something.

We must try to have *something* to say. Yet it can't be particularly new or else we'd have to say it in the House first, and it can't be particularly interesting or we'd already have said it on TV or radio. I'm always hoping that the Department will cook up something for me to talk about, something that we in the government would have to be talking about anyway.

Equally, you have to be careful that, in their eagerness to find something, they don't cook up anything too damn silly. After all,

I've got to actually get up and say it.

Most civil servants can't write speeches. But they can dig up a plum for me (occasionally) and, without fail, they should warn me of any possible banana skins.

Today I planned to make a sort of generalised speech on the environment, which I'm doing a lot of recently and which seems to go down well with everyone.

Hacker was persuaded to pose for the above photograph against his better judgement, because he was unwilling to appear 'a bad sport' in public. He subsequently had the photograph suppressed but it was released under the Thirty-Year Rule (DAA Archives)

At the City Farm we were met by a brisk middle class lady called Mrs Phillips. She was the Warden of the City Farm. My party simply consisted of me, Bill Pritchard of the Press Office, and Bernard.

We were asked to drive up to the place two or three times in succession, so that the television crew could film us arriving.

The third time seemed to satisfy them. Mrs Philips welcomed me with a singularly tactless little speech: words to the effect of 'I'm so grateful that you could come, we tried all sorts of other celebrities but nobody else could make it.'

I turned to the cameraman from the BBC and told him to cut. He kept filming, impertinent little man. I told him again, and then the director said cut so he finally did cut. I instructed the director to cut Mrs Phillips' tactless little speech right out.

'But . . .' he began.

'No buts,' I told him. 'Licence fee, remember.' Of course I said it jokingly, but we both knew I wasn't joking. The BBC is always much easier to handle when the licence fee is coming up for renewal.

I think he was rather impressed with my professionalism and my no-nonsense attitude.

We went in.

I realised that I didn't know too much about City Farms. Furthermore, people always like to talk about themselves and their work, so I said to Mrs Phillips – who had a piglet in her arms by this time – 'Tell me all about this.'

'This is a piglet,' she replied. Asinine woman. Or perhaps I should say piginine.[1]

I told her to tell me about the farm. She said that there are over fifty such City Farms, built on urban wasteland to give children who seldom see the countryside a chance to understand livestock and food production. A wonderful idea.

I was photographed with Mrs Phillips, meeting the staff, with the children and with the piglets. [*Everybody's a ham. – Ed.*] Then it was time for my speech.

There was a moment of slight embarrassment when I realised Bernard had given me the wrong speech, but that was soon overcome.

SIR BERNARD WOOLLEY RECALLS:[2]

Slight embarrassment does not begin to describe the general reaction to Hacker's speech.

There was confusion over who had the copy of his speech, I or he. I distinctly remembered giving it to him. He denied it, and demanded I look in

[1] One of Hacker's rare jokes.

[2] In conversation with the Editors.

my briefcase. There was indeed a speech for him there. And he grabbed it and read it.

[The speech has been found in the DAA archives, and we reprint it below – Ed.]

MINISTRY OF
ADMINISTRATIVE AFFAIRS

It is a very great pleasure to be here with

you all today. You know, things are

changing fast. We live in a world of change.

The silicon chip is changing our lives.

The quality of life is becoming more and

more important: the environment,

conservation, the problems of pollution,

the future of our children and our

children's children, these are today's issues.

There is quite rightly an increasing

concern about high-rise buildings and I'm

happy to reassure all of you who are Members

of the Architectural Association that

over

Yes, indeed, Hacker had insisted on reading the speech that we had put into my briefcase *after* his address to the Architectural Association on the issue of high rise buildings.

There was an embarrassed pause, while I whispered to him that *he* had today's speech. He felt in his inside pocket, found the City Farm speech, and began to read.

Unfortunately, this only increased the already considerable embarrassment.

MINISTRY OF
ADMINISTRATIVE AFFAIRS

It is a very great pleasure to be here today
at this City Farm. You know, things are
changing fast. We live in a world of change.
The silicon chip is changing our lives. The
quality of life is becoming more and more
important: the environment, conservation,
the problems of pollution, the future of our
children and our children's children, these
are today's issues.

The City Farm is a welcome and important
addition to the way of life for children in
inner cities and we in the government feel
they have a vital part to play in our children's
educational and social life, and we shall do all
we can to help this movement flourish.

Happy Birthday.

[*Hacker's diary continues – Ed.*]

After my speech I was interviewed by Sue Lawley for 'Nationwide',
surrounded by kids and animals as previously arranged with Bill.

While they were positioning everyone for the cameras, Mrs Phillips asked me if she could really rely on my support. I told her that
of course she could. She then explained that their lease was running
out at the end of the year, and they needed to get it extended.

I couldn't involve myself too directly. I had gone there to get
some personal publicity, and I'm not fully acquainted with all their
circumstances. So I pointed out that this lease was not really within
my sphere of influence, but that I would do what I could to help the

City Farm movement flourish. This I was careful to state only in the most general terms.

Then the interview began, just as a very grubby smelly child of indeterminate sex with a sticky lollipop in its mouth was placed on my knee. I tried to show pleasure instead of disgust – which I fear would have been my natural expression.

Sue Lawley asked Mrs Phillips the first question. 'Warden, I understand that the lease on this wonderful City Farm is due to run out at the end of the year.'

I could scarcely believe my ears as I heard Mrs Phillips reply: 'Yes, we have been very worried about this, but I've just had a word with the Minister, Mr Hacker, and he has indicated that he will make sure that the farm can carry on.'

I was startled and horrified, more so when Sue Lawley turned to me and asked how I was going to ensure the continuance of the City Farm.

I started out to qualify what Mrs Phillips had said, with the usual temporising phrases like 'let's be absolutely clear about this' and 'at the end of the day' and so forth, but somehow felt unable to deny what she'd said while the cameras were rolling. Instead, I heard myself saying, 'the quality of life is becoming more and more important. The environment, conservation, the problems of pollution, the future of our children and out children's children, these are today's issues.'

[*We have discovered the following series of memos that were exchanged, over the following few days, between Sir Frank Gordon, Second Permanent Secretary at the Treasury, and Sir Humphrey Appleby, see opposite – Ed.*]

A note from Sir Frank Gordon, Second Permanent Secretary of the Treasury:

H M Treasury

Sir Frank Gordon
Second Permanent Secretary

27/v.

Dear Humpy,

Saw your chap on the television
last night, cuddling a rabbit. Apparently
sees himself as the St. Francis of Tower
Hamlets. Was he after the rodent vote?

Am still desperately concerned about
the lack of parking space at Tower House.
It's now the major blockage to the
recruitment of Inland Revenue inspectors.
Any possibilities?

Yours ever,

Frank.

A reply from Sir Humphrey Appleby:

MINISTRY OF
ADMINISTRATIVE AFFAIRS

From the Permanent Under Secretary of State

Dear Frank,

The problem is solved. Two days ago I got the authority to use the 1½ acre local government site behind Tower House.
The lease is running out, and there are no utilisation plans.

Official notification will follow in due course — the wheels are in motion.

Yours ever

Humpy

27/v

A reply from Sir Frank:

H M Treasury

Sir Frank Gordon
Second Permanent Secretary

28/v.

Dear Humpy,

　　Do you mean you got an order
under section 7 subsection 3 ?

　　　　Frank.

A reply from Sir Humphrey:

MINISTRY OF
ADMINISTRATIVE AFFAIRS

From the Permanent Under Secretary of State

Dear Frank,

As our American Allies would say, affirmative. The site is currently used as a City Farm for schoolchildren. It is the very one visited by St Francis, indeed.

It can be argued that these places are unhygienic, a danger to public health etc.

I suggest you move quickly, before the lease is renewed.

Yours ever

Humpy.   28/v

A reply from Sir Frank:

H M Treasury

Sir Frank Gordon
Second Permanent Secretary

29/V.

Dear Humpy,

Very grateful for the help.
Won't it put St. Francis in a bit
of a spot? Or is that what you wanted?

Frank.

A reply from Sir Humphrey:

MINISTRY OF
ADMINISTRATIVE AFFAIRS

From the Permanent Under Secretary of State

Dear Frank,

Yes.

Yours ever

Humpy

29/v

We also discovered a brief note to Sir Desmond Glazebrook, addressed to his home at Cadogan Gardens:

MINISTRY OF
ADMINISTRATIVE AFFAIRS

From the Permanent Under Secretary of State

Dear Desmond,

I think I have found out how I can get the Minister to eat up his rice pudding.

Yours ever

J.

29/v

[*Hacker's diary continues – Ed.*]

May 29th

For some reason they didn't run the story of my visit to the City Farm in the *Standard* yesterday.

But today I got a double page spread. Wonderful. One photo of me with a duck, another with a small multiracial girl. Great publicity for me, and the department.

I was busy discussing the possibilities of visiting other City Farms – in Birmingham, Manchester, Glasgow, Newcastle. Preferably in the Special Development Areas. [*The new euphemism for marginal constituencies – Ed.*]

This happy conversation was rudely interrupted by Bernard announcing that the wretched Mrs Phillips was outside in the Private Office, demanding to see me.

I couldn't see why. Then Bernard told me that it was announced this morning that the City Farm is being closed. This was a bomb-shell.

'The lease runs out at the end of the year and it's being turned into a car park,' Bernard told me. 'For Inland Revenue Inspectors.'

Bill and I both knew what the headlines would be. CHILDREN AND ANIMALS EVICTED BY TAXMEN. HACKER RENEGES ON TV PLEDGE. That sort of thing.

I told Bernard that it simply couldn't be allowed to happen. 'Which idiot authorised it?' I asked.

He stared unhappily at his shoes. 'I'm afraid, er, you did, Minister.'

It seems that the administrative order that I signed a couple of days ago, which Humphrey said was so urgent, gives government departments the power to take over local authority land. It's known as Section 7 subsection 3 in Whitehall.

I sent for Humphrey. I told Bernard to get him *at once*, pointing out that this is about the worst disaster of the century.

There *were* two World Wars, Minister,' said Bernard as he picked up the phone. I simply told him to shut up, I was in no mood for smartarse insubordination.

'Fighting on the beaches is one thing,' I snarled. 'Evicting cuddly animals and small children to make room for tax inspectors' cars is in a different league of awfulness.'

Humphrey arrived and started to congratulate me on my television appearance. What kind of a fool does he think I am? I brushed this nonsense aside and demanded an explanation.

'Ah yes,' he said smoothly. 'The Treasury, acting under Section 7 subsection 3 of the Environmental . . .'

'It's got to be stopped,' I interrupted brusquely.

He shook his head, and sighed. 'Unfortunately, Minister, it is a Treasury decision and not within our jurisdiction.'

I said I'd revoke the order.

'That, unfortunately,' he replied, shaking his head gloomily, 'is impossible. Or very difficult. Or highly inadvisable. Or would require legislation. One of those. But in any case it could not invalidate an action taken while the order was in force.'

As I contemplated this dubious explanation, Mrs Phillips burst in.

She was in full Wagnerian voice. 'I don't care if he's talking to the Queen and the Pope,' she shouted at some poor Executive Officer outside my door. She strode across the room towards me. 'Judas,' was her initial greeting.

'Steady on,' I replied firmly.

'You promised to support us,' she declaimed.

'Well, yes, I did,' I was forced to admit.

'Then you must see that our lease is renewed.'

Sir Humphrey tried to intervene between us. 'Unfortunately, dear lady, it is not in my Minister's power to . . .'

She ignored him and said to me: 'Mr Hacker, you have given your word. Are you going to keep it?'

Put like that, I was in a bit of a spot. I did my best to blur the issue.

'Yes,' I said, 'in that, well, I shall certainly . . . you know, I didn't exactly give my word, that is, I shall explore all the avenues, make every effort, do all that is humanly possible —' Words to that effect.

Mrs Phillips was no fool. 'You mean no!' she said.

I was quite honestly stuck for a reply. I said 'No,' then that seemed a little unambiguous so I said 'No, I mean Yes,' then that seemed dangerous so I added that by no I didn't mean no, not definitely not, no.

Then – another bombshell! 'Don't say I didn't warn you,' she said. 'My husband is deputy features editor of the *Express*. Tomorrow morning your name will be manure. You will be roasted alive by the whole of the national press.'

The room fell silent after she swept out and slammed the door. An intense gloom had descended upon the assembled company – or upon me, anyway. Finally, Sir Humphrey found his voice: 'It falls to few people,' he said encouragingly, 'to be within twenty-four hours both St Francis and St Joan.'

I have got to stop this farm being closed. But how? Clearly I'm going to get no help from my Permanent Secretary.

May 30th

No story in the *Express* today, which was a slight relief. But I couldn't believe they'll let it pass.

And when I got to the office there was a message asking me to call that wretched rag.

Also, a message that Sir Desmond wanted to see me urgently. I suggested a meeting next week to Bernard, but it seemed that he was downstairs waiting! Astonishing.

So Bernard let him in. Humphrey appeared as well.

When we were all gathered, Glazebrook said he'd just had an idea. For nine storeys extra on his bank! I was about to boot him out when he explained that if they had nine more storeys the bank could postpone Phase III for seven years. This would leave a site vacant.

'So?' I was not getting his drift.

'Well,' he said. 'I was reading in the *Financial Times* a day or two ago about your visit to that City Farm. Thought it was a jolly good wheeze. And, you see, our Phase III site is only two hundred yards away from it, so you could use it to extend the farm. Or if they wanted to move . . . for any reason . . . it's actually a bit bigger . . . We thought of calling it the James Hacker Cuddly Animal Sanctuary . . .' (he and Humphrey exchanged looks) 'well, Animal Sanctuary anyway, and nine storeys isn't really very much is it?'

It was clear that they were in cahoots. But it was, unmistakably, a way out. If I gave them permission for a high rise bank, they'd enable the City Farm to stay open.

It is incredible, I thought, that I should ever have thought that Humphrey would take my side against his old chum Glazebrook. And yet, Glazebrook is not really Humphrey's type. He must be holding something over Humphrey . . . I wonder what.

Meanwhile, I had to think up some valid reasons for approving the high rise building – and quickly. The official application wouldn't be in for a while but in front of Bernard I felt I had to come up with some face-saving explanations. Fortunately, everyone pitched in.

'You know, Humphrey,' I began, 'I think the government has to be very careful about throttling small businesses.'

Bernard said, 'The bank's not actually a small business.'

'It will be if we throttle it,' I said firmly, squashing him. He looked puzzled. 'Bernard,' I said casually, 'what's one more skyscraper when there's so many already?'

'Quite so,' agreed Sir Humphrey.

'And let's announce it right away,' I continued.

So we all agreed that the high rise building will cut both ways. It will create shade for the school. Extra revenue for the public transport system. And as for privacy – well, it could be fun for people in their gardens to look up and see what's going on in the offices. Couldn't it?

'After all,' I added meaningfully, 'some extraordinary things go on in offices, don't they Humphrey?'

He had the grace to smile. 'Yes Minister,' he agreed.

7
A Question
of Loyalty

June 1st

I'm due to go to Washington tomorrow for an official visit. I should
have thought that it wasn't strictly necessary for me to be away for a
whole week but Sir Humphrey insists that it's of enormous value if I
stay there for an appreciable time so as to get the maximum
diplomatic benefit from it all.

I'm to address a conference on administration. One of the Assistant Secretaries, Peter Wilkinson, has written me an excellent
speech. It contains phrases like 'British Government Administration is a model of loyalty, integrity and efficiency. There is a ruthless
war on waste. We are cutting bureaucracy to the bone. A lesson that
Britain can teach the world.' Good dynamic stuff.

However, I asked Humphrey yesterday if we could prove that all
of this is true. He replied that a good speech isn't one where we can
prove that we're telling the truth – it's one where nobody else can
prove we're lying.

Good thinking!

I hope the speech is fully reported in the London papers.

SIR BERNARD WOOLLEY RECALLS:[1]

I well remember that Sir Humphrey Appleby was extremely keen for
Hacker to go off on some official junket somewhere. Anywhere.

He felt that Hacker was beginning to get too much of a grip on the job.
This pleased me because it made my job easier, but caused great anxiety to Sir
Humphrey.

I was actually rather sorry to have missed the Washington junket, but Sir
Humphrey had insisted that Hacker take one of the Assistant Private Secretaries, who needed to be given some experience of responsibility.

When he'd been away for five or six days I was summoned to Sir Humphrey's office. He asked me how I was enjoying having my Minister out of

[1] In conversation with the Editors.

the office for a week, and I – rather naïvely – remarked that it made things a little difficult.

It was instantly clear that I had blotted my copybook. That afternoon I received a memo in Sir Humphrey's handwriting, informing me of the benefits of ministerial absence and asking me to commit them to memory.

[*Fortunately Sir Bernard kept this memo among his personal papers, and we reproduce it here, written on Sir Humphrey's margin shaped notepaper – Ed.*]

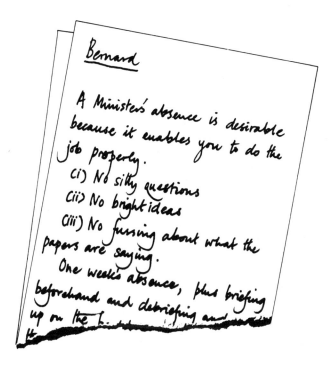

Bernard,
A Minister's absence is desirable because it enables you to do the job properly.

   (i) No silly questions
  (ii) No bright ideas
 (iii) No fussing about what the papers are saying

One week's absence, plus briefing beforehand and debriefing and catching up on the backlog on his return, means that he can be kept out of the Department's hair for virtually a fortnight

Furthermore, a Minister's absence is the best cover for not informing the Minister when it is not desirable to do so – and for the next six months, if he complains of not having been informed about something, tell him it came up while he was away

[*Sir Bernard continued – Ed.*]

Anyway, the reason behind the increasing number of summit conferences that took place during the 1970s and 1980s was that the Civil Service felt that this was the only way that the country worked. Concentrate all the power at Number Ten and then send the Prime Minister away – to EEC summits, NATO summits, Commonwealth summits, anywhere! Then the Cabinet Secretary could get on with the task of running the country properly.

At the same meeting we discussed the speech that Peter had written for the Minister to deliver in Washington.

I suggested that, although Peter was a frightfully good chap and had probably done a frightfully good job on it in one way, there was a danger that the speech might prove frightfully boring for the audience.

Sir Humphrey agreed instantly. He thought that it would bore the pants off the audience, and it must have been ghastly to have to sit through it.

Nonetheless, he explained to me that it was an excellent speech. I learned that speeches are not written for the audience to which they are delivered. Delivering the speech is merely the formality that has to be gone through in order to get the press release into the newspapers.

'We can't worry about entertaining people,' he explained to me. 'We're not scriptwriters for a comedian – well, not a professional comedian, anyway.'

He emphasised that the value of the speech was that it said the correct things. In public. Once that speech has been reported in print, the Minister is committed to defending the Civil Service in front of Select Committees.

I sprang to the Minister's defence, and said that he defends us anyway. Sir Humphrey looked at me with pity and remarked that he certainly does so when it suits him – but, when things go wrong, a Minister's first instinct is to rat on his department.

Therefore, the Civil Service when drafting a Minister's speech is primarily concerned with making him nail his trousers to the mast. Not his colours, but his trousers – then he can't climb down!

As always, Sir Humphrey's reasoning proved to be correct – but, as was so often the case, he reckoned without Hacker's gift for low cunning.

[*Hacker's diary continues – Ed.*]

June 7th

I got back from Washington today. The visit was quite a success on the whole though I must say my speech didn't exactly thrill them. I mustn't leave speeches to the Department – they give me very worthy things to say but they're always so bloody boring.

I've been met by a huge backlog of work, piles of red boxes, half a ton of cabinet papers, hundreds of memos and minutes and submissions to catch up on.

And I doubt if I can ever really catch up on it because tomorrow I go in front of a Select Committee and I've got to try to read the redrafted paper on Establishment levels beforehand. Not only read it, but understand it. And not only understand it, but remember it. And it's been written by an Under-Secretary – therefore it's not in English, but in Under-Secretaryese.

Still, at least the press did report my speech, so that's all right.

Sir Humphrey popped in to welcome me home, and to brief me about the Select Committee.

'You do realise the importance of this hearing, don't you Minister?'

'Of course I do Humphrey. The press will be there,' I explained.

[*Like many politicians, Hacker did not seem to believe in his own existence unless he was reading about himself in the newspapers – Ed.*]

'It's not just a question of the press,' he said, 'This is a scrutiny of the Department's future operation. If we were to emerge from the hearing as extravagant or incompetent . . .'

I interrupted him with a penetrating question. 'Are we extravagant or incompetent?'

'Of course not,' he replied with considerable indignation. 'But there are hostile MPs on the Committee. Especially the member for Derbyshire East.'

I hadn't realised that Betty Oldham was on the committee.

Humphrey handed me a thick folder full of papers, with red and yellow and blue tags. 'I urge you to master this brief, Minister,' he said, and told me to ask if I found any problems.

I was fed up. I'm tired and jet-lagged today. I told him that I didn't want another brief on the select committee, I only just mastered one on the plane.

'What was in it?' he asked.

That was a bit embarrassing. I couldn't quite remember. I explained that it's rather hard to concentrate on the plane, as they keep trying to serve you drinks and show you movies and wake you up.

'I'm sure it's frightfully difficult to concentrate if you keep being woken up, Minister,' he said sympathetically. He added that this was the first and only brief containing possible questions from the Committee, all with the appropriate answers carefully presented to give the Department's position.

'Are they all absolutely accurate?' I wanted to know.

'It is carefully presented to give the Department's position,' he replied carefully.

'Humphrey,' I explained equally carefully. 'These Select Committees are very important. I can't be seen to mislead them.'

'You will not be seen to mislead them.'

I wasn't satisfied. I began to suspect that the brief was not strictly honest. I pressed him further. 'Is it the truth?'

'The truth and nothing but the truth,' he assured me.

'And the whole truth?'

'Of course not Minister,' he replied with some impatience.

I was confused. 'So we tell them we're keeping some things secret, do we?'

He shook his head and smiled. 'Indeed not.'

'Why not?' I asked.

Sir Humphrey rose from his chair and announced magisterially: 'He that would keep a secret must keep it secret that he hath a secret to keep.' Then he left the room.

I was interested in the quotation, which struck me as rather profound. 'Who said that?' I asked Bernard.

Bernard looked puzzled. He stared at me, and then stared at the doorway through which Sir Humphrey had just walked.

'It was Sir Humphrey,' he said.

Sometimes I think these people live on a different planet!

[*It is significant that Hacker was not at all shocked at the suggestion that he should conceal information from the Select Committee, or indeed tell lies to it. Such lies would be regarded in government circles as white lies. There are a number of issues about which a Minister automatically tells lies, and he would be regarded as foolish or incompetent if he told the truth. For instance, he would always deny an impending devaluation, or a run on the pound. And he would always give the impression that the UK had adequate and credible defences –* Ed.]

I sat at my desk feeling utterly washed out after a night with British Airways and a day with the Civil Service, and gazed at the enormous brief that I had to master in one day.

'Why?' I wondered aloud,' are Ministers never allowed to go anywhere without their briefs?'

'It's in case they get caught with their trousers down,' Bernard replied rather wittily. At least, I *think* it was wit, but it might just have been a lucky chance.

He had kept my diary free for the whole day, so we were not interrupted. It emerged, as we went through it, that the submission that I'd read on the plane was a rehash of the report the Department produced last year. And the year before. And the year before that. Ever since 1867 probably. I pointed out to Bernard that the first sentence was enough to cure anybody of any desire to read the thing: 'The function of the DAA is to support and service the administrative work of all government departments.'

'Oh no,' he said, 'that bit's fascinating.'

I asked him how anyone could be fascinated by it.

'Well,' he said, 'if you look back to the first report in 1868, when Gladstone set up this department's predecessor, you find that the first sentence is, 'The Department is responsible for the economic and efficient administration of government.'

'Ah,' I said, 'is that what it was for?'

'Yes,' said Bernard, 'but it proved a tough remit. They were responsible for every bit of waste and inefficiency. I suppose Gladstone meant them to be. So when it got too hot they did the usual.'

'What is "the usual"?', I asked.

It emerged that 'the usual' in Civil Service terms is to secure your budget, staff and premises and then quietly change your remit. In 1906 they changed the first sentence to 'The Department exists to *further* the efficient and economic administration of Government.' This removed the responsibility.

In 1931 they got it down to 'The Department exists to support all government departments in *their* pursuit of economic and efficient administration' which pushed the responsibility on to other departments. And by 1972 they had got rid of the embarrassing notions of economy and efficiency, and since then it has said 'The purpose of the DAA is to support and service the administrative work of all government departments.' The last vestige of the department's real purpose removed in a mere one hundred and four years, and the department itself one hundred and six times its original size.

I now see why Bernard is fascinated, but I still could hardly stay awake to the end of paragraph one. Perhaps it was just the jet-lag. Anyway, Bernard reminded me that the press will be there tomorrow – so I had no choice but to get down to it.

June 8th

I had my first experience of being grilled by a Select Committee today and I didn't like it one bit.

It all happens in a committee room at the House, a large gloomy

Gothic room with an air of Greyfriars school about it. I was made to feel a bit like Billy Bunter caught with his hands in someone else's tuckbox.

Along one side of a long table sit about nine MP's with the Chairman in the middle. On the Chairman's right is the secretary, a civil servant, who takes minutes. There are a few seats for the public and the press.

I was allowed to have Bernard with me, sitting slightly behind me of course, plus Peter Wilkinson and Gillian something-or-other from the Department. (*Assistant Secretaries – Ed.*)

I was allowed to make an opening statement. I'd done my homework well, and I reiterated everything that Sir Humphrey said in his submission: namely that the Department of Administrative Affairs is run to a high standard of efficiency and does indeed support and service the administrative work of all government departments.

Mrs Betty Oldham began the questioning. She tossed her red hair and smiled a thin, mirthless smile. Then she asked me if I'd heard of Malcolm Rhodes.

I hadn't. I said so.

She went on to inform me that he is an ex-Assistant Secretary from the DAA. I started to explain that as there are twenty-three thousand people working for the DAA I can hardly be expected to know them all, when she shouted me down (well, spoke over me really) and said that he was eased out, became a management consultant in America and has written a book.

She waved a pile of galley proofs at me.

'This is an advance proof,' she announced, with a glance at the press seats, 'in which Mr Rhodes makes a number of astounding allegations of waste of public money in the British Civil Service, particularly your department.'

I was stumped. I really didn't know how to reply. I asked for a quick private word with my officials.

I turned to Bernard. 'Do we know anything about this?' I whispered urgently.

Peter said, 'I didn't know Rhodes had written a book.'

Gillian just said: 'Oh my God, oh my God!' That really filled me with confidence.

I asked who he was. Gillian said, 'A troublemaker, Minister.' Peter said he wasn't sound, the ultimate insult.

Bernard, who clearly knew even less about him than Peter and Gillian, asked what was in the book.

'We don't know.'

'Well, what do I say about it?' I whispered hysterically, aware that time was running out.

'Stall,' advised Peter.

That was a big help. I'd have to say *something*. 'Stall?' I said indignantly. 'What do you mean by it, stall?'

'Stall, meaning avoiding answering, Minister,' interjected Bernard. Like headless chickens in a crisis, these civil servants.

I gritted my teeth. 'I know what stall means, Bernard.' I was trying, not altogether successfully, to keep my temper. 'But what do you mean by sending me out into a typhoon without even giving me an umbrella?'

'An umbrella wouldn't be much use in a typhoon, Minister, because the wind would get underneath and . . .'

The Chairman called upon me at that moment, which was just as well or Bernard might never have lived to tell the tale.

'Have you had sufficient consultation with your officials?' asked the Chairman.

'More than enough,' I replied grimly.

The Chairman nodded to Betty Oldham, who smiled and said: 'Let me read you some of the scandalous facts that Mr Rhodes reveals.'

She then read me the following passage: 'At No. 4 regional supply depot in Herefordshire there are two former aircraft hangars used only for stores, but which are centrally heated to 70° Fahrenheit day and night.' [*Quoted verbatim from Rhodes's book – Ed.*] 'What have you got to say about that?' she asked.

Naturally I had absolutely nothing to say. I pointed out that I couldn't possibly be expected to answer that sort of detailed question without prior notice.

She conceded the point, but claimed that she was asking about a principle. 'What I'm asking is, what conceivable reason could there be for such appalling extravagance?'

The Chairman and the committee seemed to think I should answer. So I made a stab at it. 'Some materials deteriorate badly at low temperatures. It would depend on what was being stored.'

I'd played right into her hands. 'Copper wire,' she said promptly, and smiled.

'Well . . .' I made another guess at what conceivable reason there could be. 'Er . . . copper can corrode in damp conditions, can't it?'

'It's plastic-coated,' she said, and waited.

169

'Plastic-coated,' I said. 'Ah well. Yes.' They still seemed to want something of me. 'Well, I'll have it looked into,' I offered. What else could I say?

I'd hoped that would be the end of it. But no. It was only the beginning.

'Mr Rhodes also says that your department insists on ordering all pens, pencils, paperclips and so on centrally, and then distributing them against departmental requisitions.'

'That seems very sensible to me,' I replied cautiously, scenting a trap. 'There are big savings on bulk purchases.'

There *was* a trap. 'He demonstrates,' she continued, 'that this procedure is four times more expensive than if local offices went out and bought what they wanted in the High Street.'

I thought of remarking that you can prove anything with figures, but decided against it. Clearly he, and she, wouldn't make this claim without *some* evidence. And my experience of the DAA suggests that Rhodes was probably absolutely right anyway. So I told her that I found this information very interesting and that I'd be happy to change the system if it were shown to be necessary. 'We're not a rigid bureaucracy, you know,' I added.

This remark proved to be a tactical error. 'Oh no?' she enquired acidly. 'Mr Rhodes says that he gave these figures and proposed this change when he was in your department, and it was turned down on the grounds that people were used to the existing procedure. How's that for a rigid bureaucracy?'

I'd led with my chin there. I really had no defence immediately available to me. Again I offered to have the matter looked into.

'Looked into?' she smiled at me contemptuously.

'Looked into, yes,' I asserted defiantly, but I was losing my nerve.

'You did say in Washington last week that your department conducted a ruthless war on waste and could teach the world a lesson?' I nodded. She went for the kill. 'How would you reconcile that with spending seventy-five thousand pounds on a roof garden on top of the supplementary benefits office in Kettering?'

I was speechless.

She asked me, with heavy sarcasm, if I proposed to have it looked into. Now I was on the ropes. I started to explain that my responsibility is for policy rather than for detailed administration (which isn't true) and was saved by the bell in the form of Alan Hughes, a more friendly committee member. [*i.e. a committee member hoping for office in the government, or some other special favour – Ed.*]

Alan intervened and said: 'Mr Chairman, I think that the Permanent Secretary to the DAA is due to appear before us next week. Would he not be the appropriate person to answer these questions?'

The Chairman agreed, asked that Sir Humphrey be notified in advance. The wretched galley proofs were taken from Mrs Oldham to be shown to him.

June 9th
The headlines weren't good today.

New Allegations of Government Waste

Humphrey and I met to discuss the matter. To my astonishment he attacked me. 'Minister,' he said, 'you have placed me in a very difficult position.'

I was outraged. 'And what about the position you put me in? Here's the Prime Minister asking for economies right, left and centre, and I look as if I'm wasting everything that everyone else has saved.'

Humphrey looked at me as if I were mad. 'Minister, no one else has saved *anything!* You should know that by now.'

I knew that, and he knew that, and he knew I knew that, but the public doesn't know that. 'They all look as if they have,' I reminded him.

'Couldn't you have stalled a bit more effectively?' he complained.

'What do you mean, stalled?' I was deeply indignant.

'Blurred things a bit. You're normally so good at blurring the issue.'

If this was meant to be a compliment it certainly didn't sound like one. But apparently that's how it was intended.

'You have a considerable talent for making things unintelligible, Minister.' My mouth must have dropped open, for he continued, 'I mean it as a compliment, I assure you. Blurring issues is one of the basic ministerial skills.'

171

'Pray tell me the others,' I replied coldly.

Without hesitation he gave me a list. 'Delaying decisions, dodging questions, juggling figures, bending facts and concealing errors.'

He's quite right, as a matter of fact. But I didn't see what else he could have expected me to do yesterday.

'Couldn't you have made it look as though you were doing something, and then done nothing? Like you usually do?'

I ignored that remark and tried to get at the facts. 'Humphrey,' I began, 'if these revelations are true . . .'

He interrupted rapidly. 'If. Exactly! If! You could for instance, have discussed the nature of truth.'

Now it was my turn to explain a thing or two. 'The Select Committee couldn't be less interested in the nature of truth – they're all MPs.'

'You should have said it was a security matter,' said Humphrey, falling back on the usual first line of defence.

Completely idiotic! I asked him how HB pencils could be a security matter.

'It depends what you write with them,' he offered. Pathetic. He can't really think I'd have got away with that.

'And why on earth are we building roof gardens on offices?' I asked.

'We took over the office design from an American company that was going to occupy it. It just happened that nobody noticed the roof garden on the plans.'

I simply stared at him, incredulously.

'A tiny mistake,' he was defiant. 'The sort anyone could make.'

'Tiny?' I could hardly believe my ears. 'Tiny? Seventy-five thousand pounds. Give me an example of a big mistake.'

'Letting people find out about it.'

Then I asked him why we are heating sheds full of wire.

'Do you want the truth?' he asked.

I was taken aback. It's the first time he's ever asked me that. 'If it's not too much trouble,' I replied with magnificent condescension.

'All the staff,' he said, 'use these sheds for growing mushrooms.'

I didn't even know where to begin. So I kept it simple. 'Stop them,' I ordered.

He shook his head sadly, and sighed a heartfelt sigh. 'But they've been doing it since 1945. It's almost the only perk of a very boring job.'

I understand this argument, but it's clearly untenable in public. So next I asked about Rhodes's proposal for saving money on stationery orders. Why hadn't we accepted it?

'Minister,' said Humphrey vehemently, 'that man was a troublemaker. A crank. He had an unhealthy obsession about efficiency and economy.'

'But why didn't we adopt his proposal? It would have saved millions of pounds.'

'It would have meant a lot of work to implement it.'

'So?'

'Taking on a lot more staff.'

This argument was manifest nonsense. I told him so. He seemed unbothered.

'Disprove it,' he challenged me.

'I can't, obviously.'

'Exactly,' he replied smugly.

I stared at him. I had suddenly realised what was going on. 'You're making all this up aren't you?' I said.

He smiled. 'Of course.'

'Why?'

He stood up.

'As an example,' he said in his most superior manner, 'of how to handle a Select Committee.'

[*A week later the same Select Committee met Sir Humphrey. Mrs Oldham questioned him closely on the Rhodes disclosures and proposals. The evidence taken that day is printed below – Ed.*]

Mrs Betty Oldham: This is all very well, Sir Humphrey, but let's get down to details. This heated aircraft hangar for example.

Sir Humphrey Appleby: Indeed, I fully understand the committee's concern. But it can be very cold in Herefordshire in winter, and even civil servants cannot work in sub-zero temperatures.

Mrs Betty Oldham: We aren't talking about civil servants. We are talking about coils of wire, with plastic coats to keep them warm.

Sir Humphrey Appleby: Yes, but staff are in and out all the time.

Mrs Betty Oldham: Why?

Sir Humphrey Appleby: Taking deliveries, making withdrawals, checking records, security patrols, fire inspection, stocktaking and auditing, and so forth.

Mrs Betty Oldham: Well, they can wear gloves can't they?

Sir Humphrey Appleby: They could. It's a question of staff welfare policy.

Mrs Betty Oldham: Well, I suggest this policy is costing the taxpayer millions of pounds. (silence) Nothing to say, Sir Humphrey?

Sir Humphrey Appleby: It is not for me to comment on government policy. You must ask the Minister.

Mrs Betty Oldham: But you advise the Minister.

Sir Humphrey Appleby: I think the Chairman is aware that I cannot disclose how I advise my Minister. The Minister is responsible for policy.

Mrs Betty Oldham: All right. So we'll ask the Minister. Now then, what about those stationery requisition savings?

Sir Humphrey Appleby: That would have involved putting very considerable government patronage in the hands of junior staff.

Mrs Betty Oldham: Considerable government patronage? Buying a packet of paper clips?

Sir Humphrey Appleby: It is government policy to exercise strict control over the number of people allowed to spend its money. I'm sure you'll agree that this is right and proper.

Mrs Betty Oldham: But it's plain common sense to allow people to buy their own paper clips.

Sir Humphrey Appleby: Government policy has nothing to do with common sense.

Mrs Betty Oldham: Well, don't you think it's time that the policy was changed? (silence) Well, Sir Humphrey?

Sir Humphrey Appleby: It is not for me to comment on government policy. You must ask the Minister.

Mrs Betty Oldham: But the Minister advises us to ask you.

Sir Humphrey Appleby: And I am advising you to ask the Minister.

Mr Alan Hughes: When does this end?

Sir Humphrey Appleby: As soon as you like.

Mrs Betty Oldham: Well, let's come to the roof garden.

Sir Humphrey Appleby: With pleasure. It was part of a wide variety of roof insulation schemes which the government undertook to test, in the interest of fuel economy.

Mrs Betty Oldham: Seventy-five thousand pounds?

Mrs. *Betty Oldham.*

23. This is all very well, Sir Humphrey, but let's get down to details. This heated aircraft hangar for example.——(Sir *Humphrey Appleby.*) Indeed, I fully understand the committee's concern. But it can be very cold in Herefordshire in winter, and even civil servants cannot work in sub-zero temperatures.

24. We aren't talking about civil servants. We are talking about coils of wire, with plastic coats to keep them warm.——Yes, but staff are in and out all the time.

25. Why?——Taking deliveries, making withdrawals, checking records, security patrols, fire inspection, stocktaking and auditing, and so forth.

26. Well, they can wear gloves can't they?——They could. It's a question of staff welfare policy.

27. Well, I suggest this policy is costing the taxpayer millions of pounds. (silence) Nothing to say, Sir Humphrey?——It is not for me to comment on government policy. You must ask the Minister.

28. But you advise the Minister.——I think the Chairman is aware that I cannot disclose how I advise my Minister. The Minister is responsible for policy.

29. All right. So we'll ask the Minister. Now then, what about those stationery requisition savings.——That would have involved putting very considerable government patronage in the hands of junior staff.

30. Considerable government patronage? Buying a packet of paper clips?——It is government policy to exercise strict control over the number of people allowed to spend its money. I'm sure you'll agree that this is right and proper.

31. But it's plain common sense to allow people to buy their own paper clips.—— Government policy has nothing to do with common sense.

31. Well, don't you think it's time that the policy was changed? (silence) Well, Sir Humphrey?——It is not for me to comment on government policy. You must ask the Minister.

33. But the Minister advises us to ask you.——And I am advising you to ask the Minister.

Mr. *Alan Hughes.*

34. When does this end?——(Sir *Humphrey Appleby.*) As soon as you like.

Mrs. *Betty Oldham.*

35. Well, let's come to the roof garden. ——(Sir *Humphrey Appleby*). With pleasure. It was part of a wide variety of roof insulation schemes which the government undertook to test, in the interest of fuel economy.

36. Seventy-five thousand pounds? ——It was thought that the sale of flowers and vegetable produce might offset the cost.

37. And did it?——No.

38. Then why not abandon the garden? ——Well, it's there now. And it does insulate the roof. But we aren't building any more.

39. But you've wasted seventy-five thousand pounds.——It was the government's policy to test all the proposals for fuel saving.

40. At this fantastic waste of tax-payer's money? You agree the money was wasted? ——It is not for me to comment on government policy. You must ask the Minister.

41. Look, Sir Humphrey. Whatever we ask the Minister, he says is an administrative question for you. And whatever we ask you, you say is a policy question for the Minister. How do you suggest we find out what's going on?——Yes, I do think there is a real dilemma here, in that what it has been government policy to regard policy as the responsibility of Ministers and administration as the responsibility of officials, questions of administrative policy can cause confusion between the administration of policy and the policy of administration, especially when responsibility for the administration of the policy of administration conflicts or overlaps with responsibility for the policy of the administration of policy.

42. That's a load of meaningless drivel, isn't it, Sir Humphrey?——It is not for me to comment on government policy. You must ask the Minister.

The actual report of Sir Humphrey Appleby's evidence to the Select Committee, reproduced by kind permission of HMSO.

[*We have reprinted it in more readable form – Ed.*]

Sir Humphrey Appleby: It was thought that the sale of flowers and vegetable produce might offset the cost.

Mrs Betty Oldham: And did it?

Sir Humphrey Appleby: No.

Mrs Betty Oldham: Then why not abandon the garden?

Sir Humphrey Appleby: Well, it's there now. And it does insulate the roof. But we aren't building any more.

Mrs Betty Oldham: But you've wasted seventy-five thousand pounds.

Sir Humphrey Appleby: It was the government's policy to test all the proposals for fuel saving.

Mrs Betty Oldham: At this fantastic waste of taxpayers' money? You agree the money was wasted?

Sir Humphrey Appleby: It is not for me to comment on government policy. You must ask the Minister.

Mrs Betty Oldham: Look, Sir Humphrey. Whatever we ask the Minister, he says is an administrative question for you. And whatever we ask you, you say is a policy question for the Minister. How do you suggest we find out what's going on?

Sir Humphrey Appleby: Yes, I do think there is a real dilemma here, in that while it has been government policy to regard policy as the responsibility of Ministers and administration as the responsibility of officials, questions of administrative policy can cause confusion between the administration of policy and the policy of administration, especially when responsibility for the administration of the policy of administration conflicts or overlaps with responsibility for the policy of the administration of policy.

Mrs Betty Oldham: That's a load of meaningless drivel, isn't it?

Sir Humphrey Appleby: It is not for me to comment on government policy. You must ask the Minister.

SIR BERNARD WOOLLEY RECALLS:[1]

It was theoretically true, as Sir Humphrey claimed, that Ministers are – and were in the 1980s – responsible for policy. In practice, however, Minister's are responsible for relatively little policy because the useful life of a government is only about two years. The first year is spent learning that commitments made while in Opposition cannot be kept once they are in office: once a government gets in it has to get to grips with the real problems that actually exist, invariably connected with the prevailing economic situation which is always either appalling or catastrophic, and of which the full de-

[1] In conversation with the Editors.

tails of the horror were invariably kept secret from the nation and therefore from the Opposition.

As a new government struggles to sort out these problems it will be dependent on economists and on the Treasury. This is a trifle unfortunate – economists are always in a state of total intellectual disarray and confusion and are too busy arguing with each other to be able to advise politicians who are usually rather ignorant of economics. And the Treasury, on the other hand, has had rather a lot of bad luck with its economic forecasts over the last sixty years or so.

So, after a period of between a year and eighteen months, Ministers come to an understanding of the situation as it actually is. Then there follows about two years of potentially serious government – after which the run up to the next general election begins. At this point achievement has to be subordinated to the winning of votes – or, rather, winning votes becomes the only measure of achievement. The last two years are rather like swotting for an exam. You don't do anything new, you just try to pass.

Therefore, as he knew only too well, Sir Humphrey's claim that Ministers make policy applies – at most – to two years out of every five. This Select Committee enquiry took place, of course, during the first year that Hacker was in office.

There is one further interesting question raised by this discussion. If the Minister makes policy for two years out of five, who makes policy in the other three years? Obviously, we in the Civil Service used to fill the vacuum.

And this created serious problems during the Minister's two years of 'serious government' – which were therefore frequently absorbed in a war between the Minister's policies and the Ministry's policies.

The only time that this eighteen month vacuum did not occur at the start of a government was when a government was re-elected for a second full term with a working majority. By the mid-1980s this had not occurred in Britain for a quarter of a century. This is why it was always absurd to categorise the Civil Service as either Conservative or Labour – we always believed in, and hoped for, regular alternation of governments. This gave us the maximum freedom from control by Ministers who, if they stayed too long in office, were likely to begin to think that they knew how to run the country.

June 16th

Today I read in the papers the reports of Humphrey's appearance before the Select Committee. He's been a big help!

And we've both been called back to make a joint appearance, to sort out the mess that he made.

I called him in and gave him a bollocking.

He said he'd done his best.

I told him: 'You did your best for yourself, perhaps. But you've solved nothing. The day after tomorrow we'll be sitting there, side by side, getting the third degree from the committee. We must have proper answers – or, at the very least, the *same* answers.'

Humphrey said that we must begin by establishing what our position is.

'Very well,' I agreed. 'What are the facts?'

He got very impatient with me. 'I'm discussing our position, Minister – the facts are neither here nor there.'

Fair enough. So I asked him to outline our position.

He suggested that we choose one of the Civil Service's five standard excuses, to deal with each of their allegations. A different one for each if possible.

I had never before heard of the five standard excuses. Humphrey must be quite anxious about the situation if he's prepared to reveal his techniques to me so openly.

I made notes. I have called each excuse by the name of a famous example of its use.

1 *The Anthony Blunt excuse*
   There is a perfectly satisfactory explanation for everything, but security prevents its disclosure
2 *The Comprehensive Schools excuse*
   It's only gone wrong because of heavy cuts in staff and budget which have stretched supervisory resources beyond the limit
3 *The Concorde excuse*
   It was a worthwhile experiment now abandoned, but not before it provided much valuable data and considerable employment
4 *The Munich Agreement excuse*
   It occurred before important facts were known, and cannot happen again
   (The important facts in question were that Hitler wanted to conquer Europe. This *was* actually known; but not to the Foreign Office, of course)
5 *The Charge of the Light Brigade excuse*
   It was an unfortunate lapse by an individual which has now been dealt with under internal disciplinary procedures

According to Sir Humphrey, these excuses have covered everything so far. Even wars. Small wars, anyway.

I finished making notes, and contemplated the list. It seemed okay, if we could carry it off. But I knew I couldn't manage it without Humphrey.

I smiled at him encouragingly. 'All right,' I said, 'so it's real teamwork from now on, eh, Humphrey?'

'United we stand, divided we fall,' he replied, with a distinctly optimistic air.

I was about to start going through the list to see which excuse we could apply to which allegation, when Bernard reminded me that I had to be at the House in ten minutes for a committee meeting. 'And,' he added nervously, 'Number Ten's been on the phone. Sir Mark Spencer [*the Prime Minister's special political advisor – Ed.*] wonders if you could pop in for a drink sometime tomorrow. I suggested five-thirty.'

I pointed out to Sir Humphrey that this was *not* a good sign. Clearly the PM wants me to account for our feeble explanations to the Select Committee.

'Perhaps it *is* just for a drink,' said Sir Humphrey, with more optimism than sense.

'Don't be silly,' I told him. 'You don't get invited to drinks at Number Ten because you're thirsty.' I agreed to meet Humphrey tomorrow, and cook up a story.

'Agree our position, Minister,' he corrected me.

'That's what I said,' I replied, 'cook up a story.'

June 17th

I am very confused this evening.

At five-thirty I went to see Sir Mark Spencer at Number Ten.

Going to Number Ten is a very weird experience. From the outside it just looks like an ordinary terraced Georgian house – big, but not *that* big. But when you step inside the front door and walk along a big wide hall that seems a hundred yards long, you realise that you're actually in a palace.

It's so English, so extremely discreet on the outside. The secret of the house is that it's three or four houses knocked together, and built onto at the back as well. As a result it's pretty hard to find your own way round Number Ten. You go up and down funny little stairs, crossing from one house to another, and in no time you don't even know which floor you're on.

This, according to the drivers' grapevine, is put to creative use by the civil servants, who know the plan of the building inside out and who therefore situate their own offices in the key rooms from which they can monitor and control all comings and goings within the building. Also these are usually the nicest rooms. In fact, there is a persistent rumour that the battle for rooms goes on through every administration, with political staff fighting for the rooms nearest to

Sir Mark Spencer on his appointment as the Prime Minister's special political advisor

the PM's office – and fighting also to get the civil servants further away. But it seems that as soon as the government changes, the civil servants move swiftly and smoothly to reoccupy all the lost ground before the new Prime Minister's staff arrive.

I was escorted up to Sir Mark Spencer's office. It was a small, pokey, sparse little room, under-furnished, exactly the sort of office in which the permanent civil servants would put a temporary part-time advisor.

[*Sir Mark Spencer was the Managing Director of a well-known and popular multiple chain-store, a bye-word for efficiency and productivity, who had been brought into Number Ten by the PM to advise personally on economies and increased administrative productivity. So far, it seems, he was still struggling with the problem of getting a decent office. Presumably, if it were not for the PM's personal interest in his work, he would have been found an office in Walthamstow – Ed.*]

I'd only met Sir Mark once before. He is a big fellow, highly intelligent and with a kindly soft-spoken manner. He welcomed me warmly.

'Ah come in Jim. Scotch?'

I thanked him.

'How are things going?' he enquired gently, as he brought me my drink.

I told him things were fine. Absolutely fine. I told him that it was a bit of a shock, having Rhodes's book thrown at us out of the blue, but that now the whole situation was under control. 'Humphrey and I will be getting together this evening. We'll be able to explain everything. Nothing for the PM to worry about.'

I hoped that I was being sufficiently reassuring to Sir Mark. As I heard myself speak, however, I rather sounded as though I were reassuring myself.

I paused. But Sir Mark said nothing. He just sat still, looking at me.

I found myself continuing, and making more excuses. 'What beats me is how Malcolm Rhodes got all that information. Most of it happened outside his division. And I wouldn't mind knowing who got those advance proofs to Betty Oldham. The PM must be livid. But it's certainly no fault of mine.'

I paused again. In fact, I had really nothing left to say on the subject. Sir Mark obviously sensed this, because he finally spoke.

'What makes you think the PM is livid?' he asked, in a slightly puzzled tone.

I hadn't expected this question. I thought it was obvious. Why else was I there at Number Ten? I stared at him.

'Let's try and look at this situation logically, shall we?' suggested Sir Mark.

'Of course,' I agreed.

Then he asked me a series of questions. At first I simply couldn't see what he was driving at.

'What has the PM been trying to achieve, in public expenditure?'

'Cuts, obviously.'

Sir Mark nodded. 'And why has there been so little success?'

Again the answer was obvious. 'Because of Civil Service obstruction.'

'And are all the Cabinet committed to this policy of cutting public expenditure?'

I wasn't sure if this was an attack on me. 'I think so, yes. *I* certainly am.'

He stared at me. He seemed unconvinced. Then he said: 'If that is so, why have virtually no Ministers achieved any real cuts?'

'Rome wasn't built in a day, you know.'

181

'Wrong. It's because the Ministers have gone native.'

'Oh I don't think . . .' I paused again. I had been about to disagree. But what had I just said to Sir Mark? Rome wasn't built in a day. The standard Civil Service answer when pressed for results. But surely *I've* not gone native?

'The Civil Service has house-trained the lot of you,' he said with a little sad smile.

'Well, some of us, perhaps. But I certainly haven't been . . .'

He interrupted me. 'Look, if a Minister were *really* trying to cut expenditure, how would he react to a book exposing massive government waste?'

'Well, he'd he'd, er . . . oh!' I realised I had no immediate answer. 'It would depend on . . . er . . .' I was stuck. So I asked him precisely what he was trying to say.

He didn't answer. That is to say, he answered obliquely. 'Do you know what the Civil Service is saying about you?'

I shook my head nervously.

'That you're a pleasure to work with.' A rush of mixed emotions overwhelmed me. First relief. Then pleasure and pride. Then, suddenly, a dreadful realisation of the awfulness of what he had just revealed!

'That's what Barbara Woodhouse says about her prize-winning spaniels,' he added.

I just sat there, struggling to grasp all the implications. My head was in a whirl.

Sir Mark continued destroying me, in that kindly voice of his. 'I've even heard Sir Humphrey Appleby say of you that you're worth your weight in gold. What does that suggest to you?'

It was only too clear what it suggested. I felt deeply miserable. 'You mean . . . I've failed utterly,' I said.

Sir Mark stood up, picked up my empty glass, and observed that I looked as if I needed another Scotch.

He returned it to me, I sipped it. Then he waited for me to speak again.

'And now,' I mumbled. 'I suppose the PM is not pleased with my performance at the Select Committee because I failed to cover up the failure?'

He sighed heavily and looked at the ceiling. He was becoming impatient. 'On the contrary, the PM is not pleased because you're covering up *too well*.'

This baffled me even more.

He explained. 'You're protecting the Civil Service. You're protecting Humphrey Appleby. The PM and I are doing our level best to expose why cuts in public expenditure are not taking place – and you're helping the Civil Service to defy the Government.'

'Am I?' My brain was reeling. How *could* I be doing that?

'You were wondering where Betty Oldham got the advance proofs of that book. And where Malcolm Rhodes got the inside information.' He smiled at me. And waited. I just stared at him, blankly. 'Can't you guess?' he asked eventually, with pity in his voice.

Suddenly the light dawned. 'You mean . . . the PM?' I whispered.

Sir Mark looked shocked. 'Of course not . . . not directly.'

'You mean,' I whispered again, *'you?'*

He sipped his drink and smiled.

So that was it. Whether wittingly or unwittingly, Malcom Rhodes and Betty Oldham had been put up to this by the PM's special advisor. And therefore, in effect, by the PM.

Therefore . . . therefore what? What do I do at the Select Committee. What does Number Ten want?

'There's only one course open to you,' Sir Mark added enigmatically. 'Absolute loyalty.'

'Ah,' I said, and then realised that my worries were not fully answered. 'But, er, who to?'

'That's your decision,' he said.

I think I know what is expected of me. I *think*.

June 18th

Today we met the Select Committee and I really put the cat among the pigeons.

They started with the plastic-coated copper wire in the heated sheds. Humphrey gave the answer that he and I had agreed he would give when we met earlier today. He said that the error actually occurred before some important facts were known and that he was able to answer the Committee that no such oversight could possibly occur again.

He asked me to agree.

My answer surprised him.

'Yes,' I said. 'Sir Humphrey's reply is absolutely correct. The correct *official* reply.' He glanced at me quickly. 'But I've been thinking very deeply since our last meeting' (which was true!) 'and really there is no doubt that this committee is on to something.'

Humphrey turned and stared at me in astonishment.

'Of course there's waste,' I continued carefully, 'whatever the ex-cuses that we can always find for individual cases. You have con-vinced me that our whole attitude is wrong.'

It was clear from the expression on his face that they had not con-vinced Sir Humphrey.

Nevertheless, I took my courage in both hands, and continued. 'Ministers and their civil servants cover-up and defend where we should seek out and destroy.' Sir Humphrey was now absolutely aghast. 'I have spoken to Mr Malcom Rhodes, the author of this in-valuable book, and he has agreed to give extensive evidence to an outside independent enquiry which I shall set up.' I could see Sir Humphrey out of the corner of my eye, putting his head in his hands. 'This will examine the whole of government administration, starting with my department.'

The Chairman looked pleased. 'How does Sir Humphrey react to this?' he asked.

Sir Humphrey lifted his head from his hands and tried to speak. But no words came out.

I quickly answered for him. 'He is in full agreement. We work as a team, don't we Humphrey?' He nodded weakly. 'And I may say he's a pleasure to work with.'

Meanwhile, Betty Oldham had been thrown into a state of confu-sion. She was still trying to attack me, but there was no longer any reason to do so.

'But Minister,' she complained shrilly, 'this account of what's been going on doesn't square with what you were saying in your Washington speech about a ruthless war on waste.'

I was ready for that. In my most patronising manner I explained my position. 'Well Betty,' I said, 'I'm an old-fashioned sort of chap. I believe in things like loyalty. Whatever you say to them privately, you defend your chaps in public. Eh, Humphrey?'

Humphrey was now eyeing me as if I were a rabid dog.

'In that case,' pressed Mrs Oldham, 'aren't you being rather dis-loyal to them now?'

'No,' I explained charmingly, 'because in the end a Minister has a higher loyalty – a loyalty to Parliament, a loyalty to the nation. And that loyalty must take precedence, come what may, painful as it may be. My belief is that one is loyal to one's department and one's officials until the evidence is overwhelming. But I must now say in public what I have long been saying in private: that reforms can and will be carried out and I know that in Sir Humphrey I will find my staunchest ally. Isn't that so, Humphrey?'

'Yes Minister,' replied my staunchest ally in a thin choking voice of pure hatred.

After the meeting was over Humphrey, Bernard and I strolled back across Whitehall to the DAA. It was a lovely sunny June day with a cool breeze from the river. I was feeling fairly positive about it all, though desperately hoping that I had not misunderstood Sir Mark's intentions. It seemed to me that I had just been as loyal as could be to the PM, even though I'd upset Sir Humphrey more than somewhat.

Humphrey didn't speak all the way back to the Department. He was too angry. Bernard didn't either. He was too frightened.

In fact, nothing was said until we were back in my office. Humphrey had followed me into my room, so clearly he did have something to say to me.

I shut the door and looked at him expectantly.

'That was a big help Minister,' he began.

'I did my best,' I replied with a modest smile.

He stared at me, trying to understand why I had behaved as I had. He must have thought that I had gone out of my mind.

'You did your best for yourself, perhaps,' he said. 'So this is your idea of teamwork, is it? Most amusing, if I may say so.'

I felt I should explain. So I started to say that I had to do it, that I'd had no choice. He wouldn't listen.

'You had to do *what*? Cravenly admitting everything to that committee. Don't you realise how utterly calamitous this has been for us?'

'Not for me, I hope,' I replied.

He shook his head, more in sorrow than in anger. 'You hope in vain, Minister. The Department is up in arms – they will have very little confidence in you in future. And as for Number Ten – well, I shudder to think how the PM may react to a public admission of failure.'

I said nothing. As I sat there, wondering for a moment if I'd made a ghastly mistake, Bernard knocked and came in. He was holding an envelope.

'Excuse me, Minister, sorry to interrupt,' he said nervously, 'but here's a personal letter from the Prime Minister.'

He handed it to me. Sir Humphrey shook his head. I ripped it open. As I read it I was aware of Humphrey's voice.

'I did warn you,' it was saying. 'Bernard, perhaps you should give some thought to drafting a face-saving letter of resignation for the Minister.'

I read the letter.

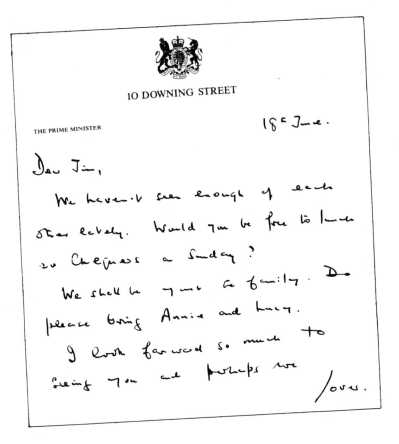

10 Downing Street
S.W.1.

The Prime Minister   18th June

Dear Jim,

We haven't seen enough of each other lately. Would you be free to come to lunch at Chequers on Sunday? We shall be just the family. Do please bring Annie and Lucy.

I look forward so much to seeing you and perhaps we could catch up on each other's news.

Then I read it aloud.

Humphrey's face was a picture of confusion. 'I don't think I quite . . .' he said, and then the penny dropped. 'A conspiracy!' he hissed at me. 'That drink with Mark Spencer!'

I just smiled. The gamble had paid off. I re-read the letter. It was a triumph. 'We haven't seen enough of each other lately . . . lunch at Chequers . . . just the family . . .' And it is *handwritten*.

'Do you know what this letter is worth, Humphrey?' I asked with quiet pride.

'I believe the going rate is thirty pieces of silver,' he replied nastily.

I shook my head. 'No Humphrey,' I said with supreme confidence. 'Integrity and loyalty have been rewarded.'

'Loyalty?' he sneered contemptuously. 'Loyalty?'

I just couldn't resist rubbing his nose in it. 'Yes Humphrey. I supported you just the way you have always supported me. Isn't that so?'

He really didn't know how to answer that. A sort of snorting noise emanated from behind his clenched teeth.

'Did you say something Humphrey?' I asked politely.

'I think,' said Bernard, 'that he said "Yes Minister."'